Developing a crush on a complicated man like Trevor Kincaid would be a mistake

Whether they were on a break or not, Isabel shouldn't give up on Roger. He might be a little gun-shy about a second marriage, but at least the marriage gun he wielded was loaded with fairly innocuous pellets. Eventually she'd convince Roger to marry her.

And that was what she wanted, wasn't it? Marriage to a man who would stick around. And happy children. She thought she could achieve that with Roger. Why, she was already halfway there if she counted Angie and RJ.

Trevor was actually a year older than Roger and he'd never been married.

She didn't think he had any kids. He was a committed bachelor, she had no doubt, and she could see why.

An enigmatic, sexy man like Trevor would surely come equipped with a machine gun.

A relationship with *him* simply wasn't safe.

Dear Reader,

Do you know these people? She thinks nothing of sacrificing an afternoon to watch her down-on-their-luck neighbors' kids. He brings a dozen doughnuts to the office on Monday morning, including several of those chocolate old-fashioneds you like and a jelly-filled Danish for the receptionist. She plans a girls' night out on the second anniversary of your breakup, because she's been there and she knows some times are still rough.

Thoughtful folks. I'm lucky enough to know a few of them. Isabel, my heroine and the second of the HEARTLAND SISTERS, is just such a people person. Sometimes she gets so caught up in helping everyone else that she forgets about her own wishes. She tells herself that her greatest desire is to make other people happy. Maybe so. But maybe she's also afraid. Will people think she's selfish? Will she try and fail? Will she try and *succeed*, and have to let someone down?

Oh, yes. I know a few Isabels.

Trevor Kincaid doesn't have any trouble striving for his goals, and he lives the kind of exciting life Isabel only dreams about. He has a few fears of his own, however, and he's missed out on the great adventure of trusting and loving another person to the depths possible in a truly committed relationship.

As with the best of couples, Isabel and Trevor have much to teach each other, and much to learn. I hope you enjoy their story.

I love hearing from readers. Please contact me through my Web site at www.kaitlynrice.com.

Happy reading!

Kaitlyn Rice

The
Runaway
Bridesmaid

Kaitlyn Rice

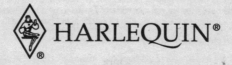

HARLEQUIN®

TORONTO • NEW YORK • LONDON
AMSTERDAM • PARIS • SYDNEY • HAMBURG
STOCKHOLM • ATHENS • TOKYO • MILAN • MADRID
PRAGUE • WARSAW • BUDAPEST • AUCKLAND

ISBN 0-373-75108-7

THE RUNAWAY BRIDESMAID

www.eHarlequin.com

Printed in U.S.A.

To a few great adults who recognize
the importance of cherishing childhood
and children:
Jim C., Jamie and Jane,
Kim and Lisa.

With a huge hug and thanks to each of you
for helping my children feel special,
in your own ways and times.

Books by Kaitlyn Rice

HARLEQUIN AMERICAN ROMANCE

Chapter One

"Toss it to me!" hollered a petite blonde as she bounced around on the lawn in front of Isabel Blume. The thirty-something dynamo had introduced herself as Peyton at the bridal shower, two weeks ago Isabel recalled, and she'd arrived at this afternoon's wedding on the arm of a George Clooney look-alike.

"Aim left and throw hard," another woman commanded from her spot near the rose-trimmed arbor. Isabel didn't remember the name of the tall redhead, but the Wichita ob-gyn had celebrated her forty-first birthday last year by touring French castles.

"Watch out, gals, this un's mine!" The husky female drawl from the back had come from the bride's college roommate, a Dallas banker who, at twenty-six, had recently been promoted to VP of her company.

From the sound of things, a person might think the women were throwbacks to a time when a nice, single gal over twenty had cause to be concerned about a dwindling pool of potential suitors. That wasn't the case here at all. Most of these women had the world by the tail: careers, lovers, numerous friends. Plans for houses and children and travel.

These women were bachelorettes, not spinsters. They were merely having fun 'as they waited for the bride to stop posing for the photographer and toss the bouquet.

Isabel wished she could get into a party mood, too, but she had never felt comfortable around so many people. She'd inherited too many of her mother's traits, she supposed. She glanced toward the waiting crowd just in time to watch Roger leave the backyard through the gate.

Where was he going?

Isabel scanned the folding chairs for Roger's two kids, then offered a quick wave when she spotted them. Maybe their dad had stepped out for a moment of quiet.

She was here as Roger's guest, of course—his cousin was the bride. Isabel didn't really know these folks. Though she'd grown up in the nearby Kansas country-side, she hadn't gone to school in Augusta. Her mother, Ella, had taught Isabel and her sisters at home. She'd kept them at home, period, always insisting that a ru-dimentary life was the better way.

How many times had Isabel wished she could trade places with any other girl in town? To attend school in a classroom with a desk her size. To accept birthday party invitations and giggle with friends over cake and musical chairs. To travel on cheerful yellow buses to the zoos and museums she'd only read about.

Even now, she'd love to switch with one of these other women for an hour—just long enough to feel her confidence. Maybe Peyton, with her obviously devoted swain, crisp gingham suit and slinky black thong sandals.

Or maybe Isabel would rather be the bride. Roger's cousin had traded vows with an Arkansas man, and the couple was moving to the Ozarks to run a shop specializing in custom-built cradles. What a dream!

When the photographer finished, the bride turned her back to the group, and the ladies resumed shouting as eagerly as the most talkative catcher behind home plate at Augusta Middle School, where Roger's son played league softball.

Isabel bit her tongue and crossed her arms in front of her. She had no business catching the bouquet. She was only standing with this group now because one of the bridesmaids had dragged her out here.

The bouquet left the bride's hands and arced over the space. Isabel watched the gorgeous pink mixture sail past the others, heading straight for her nose. At the last minute, she reached up and caught it.

Groans and chuckles filled the cool April air while Isabel righted the bouquet and inhaled its fine scent. Any magic in these flowers, she knew, was merely in the enjoyment of them.

The other women scattered into the crowd, and Isabel carried the bouquet across to the chairs, where Roger's six-year-old daughter looked as if she might burst from excitement.

"You catched the flowers," Angie hollered, jumping up from her seat to clap her hands on either side of her punch-stained mouth. "I know what that means. If you marry my daddy, you'll be my ee-bil ol' stepmother, right?"

"The word is evil, birdbrain," eleven-year-old R.J. said.

"I *said* ee-bil."

As the pair began their umpteenth squabble of the afternoon, Isabel claimed a chair near them and scowled at the bouquet.

Evil! Her sisters always told her she was too *nice*. And *old?* At twenty-seven, Isabel was hardly close to spinster age. The little girl must have heard a few too many fairy tales.

"But will you be my stepmother, Izza-bell?" Angie asked.

Isabel was still scrambling for a wise, motherly response when the groom hollered for Roger, saying he needed to join the bachelors for the garter toss.

"Where did your dad go?" she asked the kids, and when she noticed the heaping plateful of cashews and mints that R.J. was trying to hide, she confiscated it and scooped half the pile into her palm before handing it back. "R.J., do you know?" she prompted.

"He had to check his soybeans," R.J. said, speaking around a mouthful of nuts. "He said females like all this flowery junk, and since you drove your own car and all, you could stay."

Angie peered across at Isabel, her brown eyes wide and serious. "You're sposed to bring us home after the cake an' ever-thing."

Roger had warned Isabel that he had some work to finish before dark, but Isabel was surprised that he hadn't offered her the option of leaving with him.

"Sorry, he left," she shouted to the waiting men.

As Isabel watched the George Clooney guy catch the garter, then ignored the couples dancing to a few last wedding songs while she ate cake with the kids, she consoled herself that Roger's actions were probably normal for a boyfriend of over three years.

His early departure wasn't an act of neglect. He simply had chores to do. He was a good guy, overall. Honest, hardworking.

He was a *great* guy, and handsome, too. Hadn't she caught the banker eyeing him during the ceremony today? Roger's thick auburn hair and tanned, even features caught the attention of other women all the time, especially now that he'd slimmed down some. But he didn't flirt, even when the ladies invited it.

To a woman whose mother had taught her that all men were either fickle or worthless, that kind of predictability counted for a lot.

Isabel watched the crowd begin to leave, mostly in man-woman pairs. She might have the bouquet in her possession, but she'd never be the next to marry. Weddings had been too abundant in her circle lately.

She wondered if Roger had any idea that she might like to be a bride someday. His bride, and stepmother to his kids, whom she cared for on a regular basis. Whom she cared for, period.

On the way home in her car, Isabel got a clear idea of Roger's intentions. R.J. and Angie were both buckled into the backseat. As usual, R.J. had requested that Isabel turn on the radio so he could, as he'd put it, tune out the motormouth.

"I wish Daddy would marry Izza-bell," the doggedly chatty Angie murmured to her brother a moment later. "She'd be the best ee-bil stepmother in the whole U.S.A.!"

Isabel smiled at the contradiction, until she heard R.J.'s response.

"Her name is Isabel, and Dad isn't going to marry her." The boy's low voice and bold statement suggested that he thought Isabel was listening to the music.

"Izza-bell," Angie repeated, still pausing before that last syllable in the cute way she had. "But why won't Daddy marry her?" Her question spared Isabel the trouble of butting in to ask it herself.

"He's never getting hitched again. He says it all the time at home."

"He does?"

Again, Angie had voiced Isabel's own musings. She slowed her approach to Roger's farm, but worked to control her reaction. She wanted to hear the rest of this particular squabble.

"He likes her okay, though," R.J. said. "She's not exactly ugly or anything, and he says he craves adult company."

"Izza-bell isn't like other adults, dummy," Angie said. "She pushes me on the swings and plays house wif me."

"Jeez, Ange, she probably plays with you because she doesn't have her own kids or a dumb career or anything more important to do."

Ye-ouch!

Isabel pulled into the long drive at Roger's farm and

left the car idling. She'd heard enough. Roger's truck and tractor were parked in their usual places next to the cottonwoods, so she knew he must be inside by now.

She wouldn't go in. Let him pull together his own dinner and tend to his own artlessly honest kids. "If your dad asks where I am," she said, "tell him I had plans for tonight."

And she did.

Now.

Oblivious to her changed mood, R.J. said goodbye and disappeared into the house.

Angie remained in her seat. "R.J. doesn't know everything. Daddy will marry you."

Isabel turned around in the seat to peer at her tiny buddy, who must have realized she'd been listening to the backseat conversation. "What makes you think so, hon?"

"Cuz you're nice, an' Mama has a new boyfriend, anyways." The little girl sat up straight and grinned, showing off a missing front tooth. "'Sides, I'm not gonna grow up an' be like Mama. I'm gonna be like you."

"How so?"

"I don't want a dumb c'reer. I want to stay home and make stuff and play Barbies wif a little girl, like you do."

Well, ouch, again.

Isabel *had* a career. She owned and operated Blumecrafts, the home-based business her mother had started. Her handmade quilts and baskets might not earn her a doctor's or a banker's wages, but she made enough to pay her bills and then some.

And she had time left over to entertain a certain red-headed six-year-old and her outspoken older brother.

"Well, thanks, hon." Isabel got out of her car, then went around to the back to help Angie unbuckle her seat belt. "Just remember you can do anything when you grow up. Okay? Anything at all."

Angie nodded, her expression serious.

As Isabel watched her young friend get out of the car and skip up the gravel drive to the house, she realized something. The impression she'd left on those kids wasn't the one she'd intended.

Living frugally or surviving tough times or cherishing loved ones, all the more important lessons Isabel had learned over the years, weren't the ones they'd picked up. No. They'd concluded that she had time for them because she wasn't doing anything better.

Isabel drove the two miles between Roger's farm and the country house she'd inherited from her mother, then plunked the bouquet into a jug of water and changed out of the lilac georgette dress she'd designed and stitched expressly for this wedding.

An evening alone sounded nice. She hadn't ignored Roger's unspoken expectations for a long time, but the thought of doing her own thing for change gave her a strange thrill.

Maybe it was time for Isabel to wake up and seek out a little excitement on her own.

She went into her kitchen and sorted through a stack of mail, searching for a heavy envelope—an invitation to another wedding. This one was for her friend Darla's celebration, in late July.

She had met Darla over the phone five years ago, when the Colorado office manager had called to order some of Blumecrafts' nature-themed quilts to use at the vacation lodge where she worked.

They'd become closer when Darla's mother had been diagnosed with ovarian cancer about two years ago. Isabel knew the difficult length of that road. She'd nursed her own mother through the same illness.

When she found the invitation, Isabel opened the outer envelope and read the casual script on the inner one: Isabel and Guest. A first-time bride at forty, Darla hadn't planned a huge wedding. She and her live-together boyfriend, Sam, were gathering their families and close friends for a simple, outdoor ceremony at the lodge.

Though she hadn't found the heart to throw away the invitation, Isabel had already declined it. Roger hadn't been interested in the idea of a weekend away from the farm, especially in July. He'd spoken of wheat he'd need to cut, alfalfa he'd need to bale. He'd mentioned his hogs and the unpredictable Kansas weather.

Isabel had left a copy of the invitation on his rolltop desk, in case they both changed their minds, but she doubted that Roger would. He'd never ask his neighbors to look after the farm just so he could go to the wedding. He took his work seriously, and she respected the fact that he'd kept his farm going during a time when small operations were dying out.

And Isabel, too, felt tied to Augusta. She had Blumecrafts to run, a garden to tend, a house to keep. People needed her here.

But maybe she should go.

Without Roger.

He'd miss her if she was gone a week. Maybe he'd be singing a different tune when she returned—perhaps a wedding song. Even if he didn't, Isabel's sisters would be proud of her for breaking away for a while, and Roger's kids might recognize that she was more than a fun babysitter.

Darla was Isabel's closest friend outside the family, and they'd met in person only once. Back when Isabel's older sister, Callie, had lived in Denver, Isabel and her younger sister had visited Colorado for the holidays. Darla had met Isabel in the city and had taken her to lunch at a popular Mexican restaurant that boasted cliff divers. The two women had sat for hours, ordering rounds of chips and *sopaipillas* and chatting. Isabel would love to see Darla again, even if it meant traveling alone.

Before she could think of a hundred reasons not to, Isabel picked up the kitchen phone. Darla and Sam were gearing up for their busy camp season at the lodge. They might be at the office, even late on a Saturday afternoon. She dialed and listened to the phone ring.

"Burch Lodge." The man spoke quickly, as if he answered the phone that way a hundred times a day.

"Sam?"

"This is Trevor."

Ah! That voice had sounded different. Deeper than Sam's, but less growly. Sam's buddy directed the summer boys' camp at the lodge, but normally he was a law professor out in Boulder. Darla talked about Trevor all the time. He sounded like another great guy.

"Hello, Trevor!" Isabel said, excited at the thought of meeting Darla's friends.

"I'm sorry, should I know you?"

"No. This is Isabel, a friend of Darla's. Is she there?"

"Sure. Hang on."

After a moment, Darla came on the line, greeting Isabel with such patent pleasure that she found herself smiling into the phone, certain now that her decision to go was the right one.

"Hi, Darla! I have great news."

"News?" Darla said. "Didn't you go to a wedding with Roger today? What, did he finally get a clue?"

"Uh, no," Isabel said, "but I had fun and I…well, I'm feeling a need to escape home for a while. I'm coming out to Colorado, after all."

"You and Roger are coming here?" Darla asked.

"Don't sound so surprised," Isabel said. "But no. Just me."

Darla was quiet for a moment. "Didn't you say you'd never traveled this far on your own?"

"Yes, I did. Since Mom died, I've always traveled with my sisters. Sounds funny, doesn't it?"

"Oh, I understand why you'd be nervous," Darla said. "I'd be, if I'd had your childhood."

"Well, I'm ready to try something new. I'll be at your wedding," Isabel said. "I want to celebrate with you. Besides, it's time I got away from Roger and let him miss me a little, don't you think?"

"Yeah."

Something in her friend's tone caught Isabel's attention. "What's wrong, Darla?"

"My mom's going through a rough spell, Izzy. We thought the July date would be perfect, but I've been busy helping Mom. We haven't had time to plan, and the camp's starting soon." Darla paused, then dropped the bomb. "We called off the wedding."

Disappointment welled up inside Isabel, and felt so heavy in her chest that she sank down onto a kitchen chair. "But that's awful. And you must be busier still, contacting everyone to let them know." She lowered her voice. "Do you mean to say you won't be marrying Sam?"

"We're postponing the ceremony, not canceling it, and we hadn't invited many people yet. I sent your invitation early because I wanted to give you time to consider coming. I knew it'd be hard for you to get away."

Darla had been so excited about her big day. Their conversations about mothers and sickness had been overtaken by more hopeful talk about how many guests to invite, how to decorate and which foods to serve at the reception. "I'm so sorry, Darla."

"I am, too. And I apologize for the mix-up. I should've called to tell you, even though you'd already declined."

Still shaken, Isabel remained quiet.

After a moment Darla said, "You could still come for a visit, you know. I'd love to see you."

"I could help plan your wedding," Isabel said, more as a vague, wouldn't-this-be-great idea, rather than a true intention.

But Darla responded, immediately and enthusiastically. "That'd be great!" she exclaimed. "I considered asking you to be my maid of honor, but I didn't want to pressure you to come. We have plenty of room. You could stay as long as you like. Come for the summer!"

A summer-long Colorado trip. What a dream!

And then it struck Isabel: Why limit herself?

Why not take a real vacation?

Blumecrafts was doing well enough. And except for the flood last year, when three feet of muddy river water had rendered Isabel's house and workshop temporarily unusable, she'd generally worked year-round without a break.

If she caught up on her orders now, she could warn clients that new shipments would be delayed.

Her sisters would watch her house—maybe her younger sister, Josie, would move in to tend the gardens. In return, she'd get a bigger space for summer socializing and all the fresh veggies she could eat.

"What if I did come, Darla? I could free up some of your time by working in the office, or I could do legwork for the wedding. I could make favors and decorations. I could help with anything!"

"Isabel! Really?"

"Of course. This would be great for both of us," Isabel said. "I'd get the kind of adventure I've always wanted, and you'd get to keep your summer wedding."

"And Roger might get inspired," Darla added. "Are you sure you can get away from him and those kids? I know they depend on you."

Yes, they did, especially during the summertime. The school break coincided with Roger's busiest season.

But Isabel was nothing more than a casual girlfriend to Roger. Callie had pointed that out recently. And Josie had mentioned that Isabel and Roger didn't even go on dates, anymore. Their relationship had become more of a doing-what-we've-always-done type of arrangement.

As a consequence, she was nothing to Roger's kids, either. Merely a friend who cared about them.

The thought saddened her. She felt connected to the Corbetts, at least emotionally. "Yes, they do depend on me," Isabel said in a low voice. "Maybe they shouldn't."

"Right." Darla's tone was gentle, as if she expected Isabel to abandon the entire idea at this first snag.

She couldn't do that.

Isabel didn't want to hurt Roger or the kids, but she didn't want to be taken for granted forever, either. She was determined, this time, to do something different.

Something daring.

Isabel felt excitement bubble up in her chest. "You know what? R.J.'s almost twelve. He's old enough to help his dad around the farm this summer, or he can ride his bike to the local pool or to visit friends. He'll be fine."

"What about the little girl?" Darla asked.

"Angie presents more of a problem," Isabel said, thinking about options. "Her mother works sixty hours a week, but maybe she and Roger could coordinate their schedules."

"I'd think they could. She's *their* daughter."

"I know. I feel kind of bad for Angie, though," Isabel said. "Hopefully they won't argue in front of her, about who has to have her when."

"They'd do that?"

"They have before."

Darla hesitated, then said, "Things are awfully hectic around here once the camp is in session, but of course she'd be welcome, too, if it came to that."

"Didn't you tell me once that you catered to adult visitors only, during the camp weeks?" Isabel asked.

"Yes. And usually we limit ourselves to repeat guests who know the place well and don't mind the chaos. Teenage boys tend to be loud, hungry and surprisingly needy."

"Then Angie would be in the way."

"I want you to come, so we'd work something out," Darla said. "There's just one thing."

"What's that?"

"How can Roger realize all you do for him if you help him long distance, my dear?"

"I'm hoping I won't have to," Isabel said. "Besides, the idea is for him to miss me more than my child care skills."

"I'll tell you what," Darla said. "We'll just keep you locked away in our comfortable lodge until he charges out here on his trusty steed to demand your hand, your heart and your body for all time. Sound good?"

Isabel tried to imagine her even-tempered Roger doing anything so wildly romantic. Her mother would have laughed at the very thought.

But her mother had been wrong to suggest that men in general were lazy. Roger was anything but. Maybe he would come whisk her away, if he missed her enough. "Sounds wonderful," she murmured.

"It sure does. How soon can you get here?"

Chapter Two

Trevor Kincaid backed his foot off the gas pedal when he noticed the tan four-door pulled over on the shoulder, fifty yards ahead. What a rotten break, to have car trouble on this remote mountain road. Few cars traveled up here this early in the morning. Most of the tourists wouldn't be out and about quite yet, and the natives would be headed down to the cities to work. But someone else would see the car—maybe a county sheriff. Trevor was running late.

That car looked ancient. Small wonder it had broken down. The driver was probably another kid, arriving in the Colorado Rockies to live out his dream. They arrived in droves out here, with a few dollars in their pockets and no clue about where they would sleep at night.

All kinds of colorful characters lived off these less-traveled roads, too—mostly dreamers from the past who'd found the means to stay. Hell, some stayed without the means. Vagrancy was a real problem in the area.

Lord knew what kind of person might stop if Trevor didn't. He slowed further. He didn't have time to check a neglected engine, but he could give the kid a lift to the Lyons garage, along with a lecture about clean living and safe travel.

After he parked his Jeep behind the car, the driver of the sedan opened the door and got out. It wasn't a kid, though. It was a woman, mid- to late-twenties and pretty, with long dark hair.

The woman waved at him, and a gust of wind lifted her already-short skirt.

Those legs were long and sexy.

And those frou-frou shoes would have been worthless if Trevor hadn't stopped and she'd needed to hike a few miles to get help. What genius designer had decided to put high heels on flip-flops? Trevor's female students wore the dang things all the time, too, but at least their treks were across the groomed grounds of the Boulder campus.

He got out of his vehicle and met the woman between their bumpers.

"I'm so glad you stopped," the woman said as she pressed a palm to her heart. "I wasn't sure if what people said about strangers was true."

"Depends on what you've heard people say."

She studied his face for a moment, her expression pensive. She must have decided he was okay then, because she dropped her hand. "Guess that's true."

Another half second, then she chuckled. "There's not much up here, is there?"

Trevor gazed around at the scenery. They were

standing in a canyon a few dozen miles east of Rocky Mountain National Park. Massive rocks towered to the sky on their left. A brook flowed by thirty feet down on their right. The spruce and pines were especially fragrant this time of year, making the earth smell clean.

He loved this area. He'd grown up exploring this wilderness. The woman's idea of not much was a far cry from his.

Apparently, she'd understood his thoughtful perusal of the land, because she opened her eyes wide and said, "Oh, it's beautiful out here. I meant there isn't much civilization. I was hunting for landmarks, but I kept seeing that rock wall on one side and the river on the other. I'm trying to find Longmont. Do you know it?"

Oh. So she was lost, not stranded. Great, he'd give her directions and get on his way. "I traveled through there a few minutes ago, which means you're headed away from it. Turn around, and you'll see a sign fairly soon. Take a left toward town. Then you can't miss it."

She frowned. "I'm not so sure. I must be lousy at directions. I stopped a half hour ago to ask at a convenience store, and look what happened. Would you mind showing me on my map?"

That would mean he wouldn't get to the lodge as early as he'd hoped. But the woman acted so...innocent. He'd feel like a brute if he got home tonight and heard a news story about some female traveler who'd run into bad luck.

"Sure." As soon as he'd said it, the wind whirled down the canyon and picked up the bottom of that skirt again. "Maybe we'd better do this in your car," he added.

She frowned. Perhaps she was reconsidering the wisdom of trusting a stranger. Atta girl.

"I meant that you could sit in your car with the map, and I could stand outside and point out the way. I wouldn't want your map to blow off down the road."

"I figured that was what you meant," she said. "But I have a little girl napping in my car. We might wake her."

She had a child in the car? Trevor was oddly disappointed to hear it, but even more glad he'd stopped.

The woman bit her bottom lip, her brows lowering. "I could take the map to your car," she said after a moment.

"That'd work."

The woman teetered in her shoes as she crossed the gravel. She opened her car door, and Trevor tried not to watch those legs as she leaned in to grab the map. Gently she closed her car door again, then went around to the Jeep's passenger side.

She wanted to get in?

Man, she was gullible. Trevor considered giving the woman a safe-travel lecture, but instead simply opened his door and slid into the driver's seat.

"I can't believe Angie conked out this early in the day," the woman said after they'd closed themselves inside. "We had a long drive yesterday, and she resisted my wake-up call this morning."

Trevor studied the woman's face again, wondering if she could be sleeping through the reports of kidnappings, molestations and robberies that dominated the news every day. He could think of several things this woman had done wrong this morning. She'd left her little girl alone in an unlocked car, for one.

Maybe she was from some quiet little burg where nothing bad ever happened. "Where're you coming from?" he asked.

"Augusta, Kansas, about twenty miles east of Wichita." She shrugged. "It's a small town, but it was in the news last year when a good portion of the town flooded. The president declared our county a national-disaster area."

A national disaster sounded bad enough.

"Were you and your husband affected?" he asked.

"I'm not married." Briefly she lifted her ringless hand. "But yes, my house was damaged. I had to move out for a few months, until my family and I finished repairs."

Not married. That explained some of it. Most husbands would have coached this reckless optimist about highway safety.

Ignoring the twitch in his libido at the new knowledge of her single status, Trevor took the map from the woman to study it.

Single or not, she was merely traveling through.

"You are so considerate to help me," she said. "Roger told me I should stay home. He actually said I was too naive to travel alone. I told him to bug off."

This Roger sounded sharp. Trevor knew he had no business asking, but he was curious. "Who's Roger?"

The woman appeared to be startled by the question.

"Roger's my, uh, neighbor. And Angie's father." She nodded. "He lives down the road a couple of miles.

Anyway, Angie's mother remarried recently, which surprised everyone since she'd known the guy all of a month. She'd taken time off to spend the summer with her kids, and suddenly that plan changed. Angie was heartbroken, so of course I brought her with me."

Trevor knew that story. Too many people had kids and discovered later that it would take eighteen years to raise them. After murmuring his agreement that bringing the child was the right thing to do, he started detailing the best return route to Longmont.

"I truly appreciate this," she said as she took her map from him moments later.

"It was nothing."

"You're a gentleman. Thanks." She reached across the seat to pat his shoulder. But the touch was too soft. Trevor's body responded as if it were a caress.

She must have felt that zing of attraction, too. She stared at the point of contact, then frowned and snatched back her hand.

Trevor met her gaze as an awareness flowed between them. He'd noticed her, sure enough.

Legs. Eyes. Warmth.

Now he knew she'd noticed him, too.

He tensed, willing away his body's immediate and senseless response. It'd been a while, and she was sexy.

And a complete stranger, headed down the road in the opposite direction. Their paths had crossed for a few minutes. That was all. He hid his crazy regret behind a grin. "No problem."

He was already too late to worry about the time, so Trevor decided to maintain his gallant image. He jumped out of the Jeep to run around and open her door for her. "Have fun in Longmont, doing whatever," he said as she stepped onto the gravel shoulder.

"Thanks. And you have—" she gazed up the highway with a thoughtful frown, then refocused on him and shrugged "—a good life, I guess."

Trevor watched to make sure she got in her car and turned around, then started his Jeep and drove away to do exactly as she'd suggested.

Less than ten minutes later, he sped up the drive that led to the Burch ranch. Although Sam's parents had run a small-scale cattle operation here when he was growing up, their more enterprising son had added the lodge and guest cabins soon after taking over.

For the past three years Trevor had used part of his summer hiatus to come up here and direct a summer wilderness experience for teenage boys. He loved it, even if the precamp organization was a chore.

As he parked in front of the main lodge, he was pleased to see the front door open. That had to be Sam inside. Darla should be returning from Greeley this morning, after spending several days with her sick mother.

A gravelly voice drifted out from the back as soon as Trevor walked through the door. "You're late."

"Oh, I know. I stopped to help some woman out on the county road."

"Car trouble?" Sam appeared in his office doorway, sipping a cup of coffee.

"Just hopelessly lost in some rattletrap car." Trevor's eyes were glued to Sam's cup. "Any of that left?"

When Sam nodded, Trevor crossed to Darla's work area to pour himself some. He took a sip and winced. Sam might be a master at mixing protein meal for his cattle, but he couldn't remember how many scoops of coffee to put in a pot. Today he'd overshot by about two.

"Problem?" Sam scanned Trevor's face.

"This is fine."

Sam leaned his gaunt frame against the door sill. "You are really, *really* late. What'd you have to do, draw the woman a detailed map of the entire state?"

"No, I showed her the way on *her* map. That's all."

Sam held his gaze, then one side of his mouth lifted. "Must've been a looker."

"What makes you say that?"

"You're surly."

Trevor lifted his cup. "Nah, caffeine just hasn't had time to take effect."

"This is more than a normal morning grump. If you hadn't been interested in this woman, you'd be telling me all about what happened on that highway." Sam narrowed his gaze, studying him. "I'm thinking she was a red-hot redhead."

Ignoring him, Trevor took another sip of coffee and repressed the grimace when it went down.

"Exotic looking? Black hair?"

He didn't bat an eyelash.

"A blond princess?"

"More like a sleeping beauty," Trevor blurted. "She spoke openly to me, as if I were her brother or husband, and she was almost abnormally naive."

"And you liked her."

Trevor rolled his eyes. "Lord, Sam. Is this junior high?"

"Was that a yes, my cynical friend?" Sam's tanned cheeks formed two deep crevices when he smiled.

Trevor scowled. Sam had been the world's biggest cynic until he'd fallen for Darla. Now he'd decided he had some obligation to pull Trevor into romantic bliss alongside him. The guy had been nudging him toward women constantly, and he'd been way too interested in Trevor's weekends.

"Did you get her number, bud?"

Sighing, Trevor strode into his office.

"What about her name?" Sam asked from beyond the wall.

"Just settle yourself down, Sam. She was a tourist. I'll never see her again."

Sam fell silent, thank God.

Trevor set the cup on top of his file cabinet and pulled out a topographic map, refusing to think about the woman another second.

He'd never been the type to start up with anyone he couldn't afford to know well. His parents had been expert at that—between the two of them they'd been married six times. Several of those marriages had lasted less than a year, and several had produced children.

Trevor had eight stepsiblings between the ages of two and his own thirty-two. Except for the toddler, they all had commitment issues.

Not him, though. He stuck with long-term, noncontractual relationships with women who appreciated his realistic view of marriage. He'd been with Martie for four years and Christina for three. Chris had moved on five months ago, and Trevor hadn't found his next serious girlfriend, yet.

But he would. And they'd have fun and no regrets.

Clearing a spot on his desk, Trevor moved his cup there, then carried the map around to sit and study it. Five college-age counselors would be arriving in three days, requiring a week of intensive training. The following Monday, twenty-six younger boys would arrive, and those were merely the first-session campers. By the end of the next seven weeks, ninety-six boys in various stages of adolescence would have rotated in and out of here. As director of the camp, Trevor needed to be ready.

He lifted the map, forcing himself to think about day hikes and climbing excursions.

"Hey, Trev?"

"Yeah."

"What color was that rattletrap?"

He froze in his seat for a moment. Then he got up and walked out to the front office, where Sam stood gazing out the screen door. A tan car was pulling into the drive. Trevor watched it slow to a stop behind his Jeep.

When that shoe hit the ground beneath the car door, he knew it was her. Maybe she was lost again.

"Sam, I'll give you twenty bucks to go out there and give her directions to Longmont. I'm behind on work."

Sam didn't answer immediately. Probably because he was preoccupied, watching the leggy brunette get out of the car. "Your sleeping beauty?" he asked.

"She's not mine, but yeah."

"She doesn't look lost now." Sam's chuckle got on Trevor's nerves.

"She said she was going to Longmont," Trevor said.

"Darla's friend is arriving this weekend sometime," Sam reminded him. "Isabel Blume? From Kansas?"

Isabel Blume, from…Kansas.

The lost woman was Darla's good friend? Trevor would never have suspected. Darla wore leather boots, sturdy jeans and a short haircut that'd require little fuss while she worked around the ranch. She was as good as Trevor and Sam at following a trail and better at fires and fishing.

Trevor couldn't imagine the lost woman doing any of those things. Hadn't Darla said her friend was coming to help wherever she was needed, so Sam and Darla's dadgum July wedding could be saved?

"Your fiancée didn't tell me her friend was so…"

So, what? Friendly? Sexy?

Distracting?

"…green."

Sam had already headed outside. Trevor watched him step off the porch to shake the woman's hand. He watched her smile that same, openly friendly smile. Then he watched her skirt flutter up again.

He'd have to be careful to keep his thoughts off those legs and on the safety of the camp kids.

He'd also have to discourage any more electrified touches or lingering looks. It might be all right to entertain sexual thoughts about a woman he knew he'd never see again, but in the real world, this one wasn't his type.

Too dewy-eyed. She'd want the white picket fence, the scruffy dog and two children—a boy and a girl if it worked out, but of course she'd adore whichever she got.

Trevor knew that story, too. It had always read like pure fiction to him.

Besides, he had other things to worry about. The ninety-six boys whose parents had paid for this camp deserved his undivided attention. Those kids would learn nothing good from watching their camp director engage in a dalliance with some sexy tourist.

In fact, he'd love to teach them the opposite: that a man should be strong enough to wait for a healthy relationship with a woman he admired.

There went her skirt again.

Okay, so he did admire her legs.

"What in blazes is she doing wearing a skirt to a Colorado mountain lodge, anyway?" he complained to himself just before he shoved his way out the screen door.

"IT IS YOU!" Isabel said as soon as she saw her highway rescuer appear outside. "I knew that Jeep was familiar."

"Thought you were headed to Longmont."

"I was. I mean, I did go through there." She glanced out toward the road. Hadn't Darla told her she would pass through Longmont? "I was told I had to, to get here."

The trill of a cell phone interrupted.

"That's mine," Sam said, digging it out of his shirt pocket. "Could you help her with her bags, bud? We're putting her in the Ripple River room, up at the house."

Isabel watched him put the phone to his ear and walk toward the far end of the porch.

"You were past Longmont when I saw you, only a few miles from here," the younger man said, returning to the conversation Isabel would have been happy to forget.

She felt silly about getting lost, but this had been her first time to travel so far without her sisters to help navigate. Considering the non-map-reading child she'd had for company, she'd done all right to lose her way only once in almost six hundred miles.

"You must have made a loop back around."

"Must have." She stuck her hand out. "Isabel Blume, from Kansas." She paused, then said, "Well, I guess you know quite a bit about me already. But we didn't trade names."

He pressed his hand into hers, his grip firm and warm.

"Trevor Kincaid." He broke the clasp immediately.

"You're Trevor?" She might have recognized his voice if she'd been expecting to meet someone she knew out on that highway. But who'd have dreamed that a law professor would be so strong and rugged looking?

But then, Darla had told her that Trevor was also an avid outdoorsman. And that he was deadly serious at times and a load of fun at others.

Come to think of it, Isabel knew a lot about him already, too. And judging from the things that Darla had said, she was going to like him. "I don't know if you remember, but we spoke on the phone once. It's great to meet you in person!"

"Mmm-hmm." He backed up a step. "If you'll pop the trunk, we can unload."

Whoa! What had just happened? Isabel's enthusiastic greeting had been met with a distinct coolness.

She would disregard the snub. Perhaps she'd imagined it. "Old-fashioned car, old-fashioned opener," she said, handing Trevor her trunk key.

"If you'll help me grab some bags, we can probably do this in one trip." Trevor opened the trunk, stared inside and added, "Or maybe not."

She had brought a lot. In addition to her own luggage, there were Angie's smaller suitcases and two boxes of toys. Isabel had designed a quilt to give Sam and Darla as a wedding gift. That was in another box.

Everything inside this trunk was necessary. Isabel ignored Trevor's attitude and helped him unload. They set the garment bag and suitcases on the ground, then stacked the boxes beside them.

When they got down to Angie's pink floral suitcases, Trevor took them out, his expression puzzled, and slammed the trunk lid.

Did he think those cases belonged to her? "The Barbie cases aren't mine," Isabel said. "They belong to Ang—"

"Shh! Did you hear that?"

She had. It had been a soft, high-pitched sound.

"Could be one of the calves." He peered toward the east.

Isabel listened again, then glanced at the car window. "No, that's Angie. The slam of the trunk lid must have awakened her."

Sure enough, the little girl's head poked up in the

seat, and her face soon appeared in the window. "Izza-
bell, can I come out now?" she bellowed.

"I can't wait until she sees how gorgeous this place
is," Isabel said as she walked around the car. "She
missed seeing the mountains as we approached Denver."

Opening the door, Isabel grinned when Angie
emerged. With tangled red hair and sleep creases
pressed into one cheek, she was still adorable. "Come
here, hon." Isabel took the little girl by the hand and led
her to where Trevor waited.

He bent down to speak to the child. "Hi, Angie. I'm
Professor Kincaid," he said. "Would you like to see
some hummingbirds?"

Angie nodded.

He turned to point at a massive pine tree, off near a
footpath into a wooded area. "See those feeders
hanging from the limbs? There are usually several birds
hovering around them. You can see them better from the
path. Go take a look, if you'd like."

Angie headed in that direction. When Isabel started
to follow her, Trevor caught her eye. "She'll be within
sight. Let her go."

After Angie had skipped away, he asked, "Why is
she here?"

"I told you about that on the highway. Remember?"

"Not really."

Isabel squinted at him, thinking he'd changed since
their first meeting. She explained again in more detail,
about Angie's mother's surprise announcement that she
was remarrying, and the argument that had followed

between Roger and his ex about what to do with Angie while all of the adults in her life followed other pursuits.

"I didn't want Angie to feel as if she was nothing but a bother, so I brought her with me," Isabel finished, shrugging. "Darla knew I might have to bring her. She suggested it, actually."

"And you said Roger was…who?"

"My neighbor," Isabel said, feeling deceptive. But her status with Roger confused even her. Her sisters had convinced her to break up with him for the summer. Josie had advised her to talk to every man she met so she could find out exactly how wrong their mother had been about the entire male population.

Flexing her flirt muscles, she'd called it.

Big sister Callie had said almost the opposite—that Isabel should discover what it felt like to be on her own for a while.

Recognizing the wisdom in both of her sisters' advice, Isabel had declared a summer of independence from Roger.

His response? "Do what you have to do. I'll be here when you get home."

So she wasn't with Roger, exactly, even though she still hoped he'd propose when she returned from this trip.

Angie hollered that she couldn't see any birds, so Isabel and Trevor started toward the path. "I'd forgotten you had a kid in the car at all," Trevor said on the way. "Aren't you staying until Sam and Darla's wedding?"

"Yes, I am."

They reached Angie, and Trevor bent down near the child to point out a couple of fluttering shapes. "Those are hummingbirds," he said. "You have to stand real still, and watch them a few minutes. Then you'll see."

"Oh, those! They look like big ol' bugs!"

"I know they do at first. But keep watching them."

He stood up and scowled at Isabel. "She's staying all summer, too?"

She studied the tiny row of dimples that had formed above his eyebrows. "No. When Angie's mom returns from her honeymoon in a few weeks, she'll fly through Denver. We've already planned to meet at the airport, and she'll take Angie home."

Trevor kept staring at her. The man might be moody, but he had great eyes. She hadn't figured out their color yet. Gray? Green? And despite his efforts to hide it, his gaze held a reluctant interest in her that was enticing.

She'd have to be careful around him. He seemed… dangerous.

"I called Darla at her mother's house early yesterday morning to tell her about it," Isabel said. "Guess she got busy and didn't pass along the message."

"But starting next Monday, we'll be running an orienteering camp up here," Trevor said. "The boys are older, between twelve and eighteen, and expect to learn real wilderness skills. We explore offsite part of the time, but when we're on property we attempt some dangerous things. We work with gear—fish hooks and climbing apparatus. Fire. Surely you realize a younger child will be in the way."

Angie moved closer to Isabel, pressing her face into

the side of her waist. After glaring a warning at Trevor, Isabel rubbed the girl's arm. "It's all right, hon," she said. "Darla and I really did discuss this yesterday. She assured me that we'd work out any problems."

Angie came out from hiding and put her hands on her hips. "Is he jist an ee-bil ol' Grinch?" she asked in a normal voice.

Isabel stifled a smile. He'd deserved that. Though Trevor had valid concerns, he shouldn't voice them in front of Angie. "I think the word you're looking for is grouch," she corrected, without bothering to lower her voice, either.

He deserved that, too.

Trevor shifted his gaze between Angie and Isabel, then shrugged. "Okay, then. Leave the luggage where it is and come inside."

Chapter Three

Isabel and Angie followed Trevor through a large office, then into one of several smaller rooms off to the side. He waved toward a bench that ran along a long, windowless wall. "Have a seat," he said.

"Wow, look at that tree chair!" Angie exclaimed, eyeing the bench constructed from a rough log. She ran the length of it twice, then plopped down in its middle and ran her hand along the smoothed seat.

Isabel remained near the doorway, watching as Trevor strode behind a cluttered desk, sat down and picked up a large map.

She sat on the bench near Angie, feeling confused. "Why are we here?" she asked. "Didn't Sam mention the Ripple River room?"

"Yes, and I started to tell you bef—"

The bench squeaked loudly, drawing their attention. Angie was bouncing on her bottom. Isabel knew why. She lifted her brows and turned to Trevor. "Rest room?"

"Out in the main office." After a subtle sigh, he dropped the map and got up to point out the way to Angie.

When he returned, he explained, "The Ripple River room is small, and really meant for one person." He sat in his chair, then leaned back, dropping his elbows on the armrests and linking his fingers. He stared at Isabel, his expression sober. "I'm not sure where to put you, considering this change. We'll have to wait for Sam."

Although he didn't *say* she'd caused trouble by bringing Angie, he implied it.

Oh, man, did he imply it.

"I explained that Angie is only here because of special circumstances."

"I know."

A minute later, Angie hopped back into the room on one foot. Kids that age could amuse themselves so easily, Isabel thought. Taking an extra notebook and pen from her purse, she handed them to the little girl.

He'd see. Angie would be no trouble at all.

Trevor returned his attention to his map, and the office grew quiet again. Isabel heard only the occasional rattle of his map, the scratch of Angie's pen against the paper and the tick of the clock.

She perused the Lonely Stars quilt tacked to the wall behind Trevor's head. All of her quilts were her own unique designs. She'd done this one in rich indigo blues and deep forest greens, with stars in a silvery white.

"I sold your quilt to Darla last year," Isabel said to break the uncomfortable silence. "She said it was your Christmas present."

Trevor looked up at her, then turned in his chair to scrutinize the quilt, seeming almost surprised to discover it there against his office wall. "That's right, you have some sort of crafts business, don't you?" he said. "I'd forgotten how Darla knew you."

Success! He'd sounded halfway friendly again.

She'd keep talking to see if it helped. "Actually, my mother started Blumecrafts when I was a baby, and built it up in catalog sales. She died four years ago, but I kept the business going."

She gazed at the quilt, wondering if he would appreciate the artistry and work she'd put into it.

He turned back around and leveled a sober stare at her. "You make a decent living, selling these quilts?"

"I do fine, especially since we've put the catalogs on the Internet. I also sell handmade baskets and some accessories—my hand-pieced leather handbags were a hit on the West Coast last year." She lifted her chin. "You can't buy Blumecrafts items at your average retail store."

He'd nodded all the way through her explanation, but as soon as she quieted he said, "I expected you to be older."

What did her age have to do with this conversation?

Isabel wondered if the man was ever impressed, and why she cared one way or another. "I'm old enough."

That map must be incredibly interesting, because he started reading it again.

"Do you have some kind of problem with me?" she asked.

His eyes never left his map. "No."

"No?"

He flicked a glance toward her feet, of all things.

She slid them farther under the bench and waited for

him to look at her. After a drawn-out moment, he did, and those forehead dimples deepened.

She shrugged, soliciting an answer.

"You want honesty?"

"Absolutely."

He set down his map and watched her a moment, and only the clock's tick and the scratching of Angie's pen filled the silence.

"Here it is. Sam and Darla's normal duties here at the lodge are time-consuming. The wedding planning and the camp add more work." He nodded toward Angie, who was busy drawing and didn't notice. "You should've realized you were putting Darla on the spot." He paused, then added, "But of course that's none of my business. So—" He shrugged. "No."

Isabel wasn't going to turn her car around and drive her little friend all the way home, especially since Darla had said it would be fine to bring her.

She glanced at Angie. The little girl was entertaining herself beautifully, drawing a picture of the Grinch with a short haircut like Trevor's. Isabel wanted to tell Angie to add the row of eyebrow dents.

"I'll keep her with me," she said to Trevor, instead. "If I'm busy in the office, she can color or play with some of the toys she brought."

Trevor folded those strong hands and studied the ceiling for a long while, no doubt thinking hard about his reply. "But you're here to help *Darla*," he finally said.

Isabel shook her head. "And?"

Trevor gave Isabel the same look R.J. sometimes

gave Angie—as if her question had been so ridiculous, it was hardly worth answering. "And Darla works her buns off."

Isabel knew Darla worked alongside Sam, handling everything from branding cattle to managing the guest accounts. But she was paid to do so, and Sam was her fiancé, to boot. This whole place would soon become partly hers.

Isabel had figured she could help wherever she could and stay out of the way otherwise. After all, she was volunteering here this summer.

"I can handle whatever Darla needs me to do and still keep an eye on Angie."

Trevor's gaze fell from her face to her chest and lingered, then traveled down her legs. His scrutiny stopped on her sandals again.

Isabel stared at him, waiting for him to finish his inspection. When he raised his gaze to meet her narrowed one, he blinked a couple of times. "Unless you sit out there in Darla's office every day, the chores are mostly outside." He lifted a single eyebrow. "Filth. Bugs. Sweat. You'll hate it here."

For twenty-seven years, Isabel had lived in a country house that hadn't been air conditioned until very recently—her eccentric mother hadn't believed in it. Isabel had learned to work a garden when she was six, and she'd walked the distance into town from the age of eight.

She shook her head. "I'm not afraid of dirt or work."

And she wasn't intimidated by Trevor Kincaid.

Funny. She'd liked him out on that highway. He'd

been considerate to help her, and he'd put up with her nervous babbling. First impressions could be so wrong.

He stared past her head. "Did you notice? She brought a friend."

Isabel was baffled by the statement until she realized he was talking to Sam, who had arrived in the doorway.

She turned around in time to see Sam's eyebrows shoot up. His coppery eyes focused on Angie, then Isabel, then Trevor again. "Let's talk outside, bud."

Trevor slid off his seat and stalked out of the room behind his buddy. When Isabel heard their footsteps stop on the porch, she got up and crossed to the doorway, wishing she could hear their conversation.

As soon as she stood up, however, Angie popped up off the bench, too, and asked if she could get a drink from the water cooler out in the reception area.

Damn.

Taking the little girl by the hand, Isabel led her out to help her fill a paper cone. A moment later, Sam returned. Alone.

"Sorry I was gone so long," he said. "It was Darla on the phone, telling me about her mother's visit with the oncologist. She also explained the situation with your friend. It slipped her mind until I told her you'd arrived." He shook his head. "Our bustling summer's already taking its toll on her."

"I am so sorry to hear that," Isabel said. "And I hope we haven't caused too many problems."

"What problems?" Sam asked, extending her the graciousness she'd sought from Trevor. "You have a choice to make, though. The Woodland room, here at the lodge, is vacant now. It's big enough for several people. Only problem is, the counselors and camp kids meet to party in the community room next door sometimes. It can get loud."

"And the other choice?"

"There's the spare bedroom up at the house. It's small, you'd be a little squeezed with an added cot, but the little girl might feel more at home."

"Where's Trevor staying?"

"After the camp starts, he'll stay at the lodge."

"Well, Angie and I would love to stay at the *house*."

Sam shoved backward out the screen door. "Follow me," he said, his lazy grin making Isabel feel much better. "It's a bit of a walk. I'll have Trevor grab your things and drive them over."

Isabel frowned. "But weren't we going to carry it?"

"That was before I knew you had luggage for two," Sam said, in a way that didn't make her feel as if she had messed up.

Isabel didn't want to be waited on, especially by Trevor. "If you'd give me directions to the house, I could load it back up and drive it over," she suggested.

Sam glanced at the boxes, bags and cases lining the drive. "We'll get them, really. I insist."

Isabel gave in.

As they made their way down a wood chip path lined with evergreen trees, Angie skipped along, singing a made-up song about hummingbirds. Isabel knew she should be enjoying herself, too. She was too upset.

She'd come with such high hopes. Bringing Angie along for a few weeks had seemed a minor snag. Trevor had burst her bubble in no time. She'd give her brand-new shoes and gingham suit to know what he'd said about her out there on that porch.

The woods opened out to a circular drive, and beyond that sat a house with tons of windows. Sam led Isabel in through a side entry. "This is a shortcut to your room," he said. "If you'll find me at the lodge after you're unpacked and rested, I can show you around. We have snacks in the kitchen and in the community room." He glanced at Angie. "There's plenty for a kid to do."

After turning down a hallway containing some beautiful wildlife prints, Sam opened another door. "This is the Ripple River room. Hope you'll be comfortable."

As Isabel had suspected, her own Ripple River quilt lay on the full-size bed. She was thrilled to see the way Darla had decorated the rest of the room using colors from her design. A small, natural wood desk and matching rocker invited relaxation, and two windows provided incredible views of the trees.

"This is gorgeous. Thanks." Impulsively, Isabel gave Sam a quick hug before he left her and Angie alone.

Trevor walked in two minutes later, his arms bulging from the weight of the two largest suitcases. Angie had already flopped down on the floor to watch cartoons on a wall-mounted television.

"Thank you," Isabel said as he set them inside the doorway. "I'll help you bring in the rest." She started to follow him out, but he stopped and turned around.

"Relax. Sam's helping me."

The set of his jaw said the rest.

Had Isabel gone through a reality warp out in the

plains of western Kansas? She was the woman who took care of everyone around her. Always had. Always would. Why were these men expecting so little of her?

She didn't like it. As soon as possible, she'd make it clear that she was here to help.

She opened one of her suitcases and got busy, pretending she didn't notice when Sam and Trevor came and left again. Forty-five minutes later, she'd finished unpacking and setting up the room. She turned off the television and took Angie with her to find Sam, for that tour.

The offices were vacant. Isabel led Angie through the same hallway that led to the bathroom. Halfway down, they ran into a middle-aged woman with a laundry cart, who introduced herself as Edith, the head housekeeper. She said she thought Sam might be checking the bus at the side of the lodge, and directed Isabel and Angie to follow the exit signs.

On their way, they passed by the laundry room, where Angie saw an electronic game that had been shoved into a corner. "Hooh! I love this game," she said, galloping into the room to take a closer look. "Can I play? The Git-n-Go has it, and R.J. never gives me a turn."

"You don't want to see the kitchen or community room?" Isabel asked. "Sam said they have snacks and other games."

"I want to play *this* game!" Angie said, her brown eyes pleading.

Isabel studied the game, which appeared innocent enough. Some thoughtful person had even left a bowl of tokens on the floor next to it. She glanced over her shoulder and realized the housekeeper was waiting to make sure they found their way out.

"Of course she can play," Edith said. "Go on out and talk to Sam, if you want. I'll be working in this hallway, anyway."

Both women smiled at Angie's joyful whoops. "You be good," Isabel told her young friend. "I'll go tell Sam we're unpacked but not ready for a tour, then come right back to see how you're doing."

The little girl had already plugged a token into the game and didn't answer.

"Angie," Isabel said, and waited until the little girl had stopped and turned around. "Did you hear me?"

"Yes, Izza-bell. I'll be good and teach that ee-bil ol' grouch a lesson."

Apparently, Isabel wasn't the only one with that goal.

Right outside the laundry room, she found the exit and walked out onto the opposite side of the porch. Trevor's Jeep was parked in the drive again, but Sam was nowhere in sight. As she stepped off the porch to search for him, Isabel felt a rush of excitement about being in such a great place, so far away from her everyday world. The warmth of the sunshine on her bare arms felt good, and the spicy scent of the pine trees enveloped her.

Isabel paused, hearing rushing water somewhere nearby. That was right. Darla had told her the property backed on to the St. Vrain River. She couldn't wait to explore.

But Sam wasn't out here. A big blue bus was parked adjacent to the building, and beyond that Isabel could see a dirt road and a gated pasture. She'd just turned around, thinking she would wait to talk to Sam later, when his voice drifted to her from the direction of the lodge.

Isabel hastened around the rear corner of the building, until Sam's next statement stopped her in her tracks. "That doesn't matter, bud. She's Darla's guest, and she drove all the way from Kansas to help out."

He called Trevor "bud," didn't he?

They were together, talking about her!

"She got lost on that highway with a map and help, and she thought nothing about getting into a stranger's car. I'm only saying that she's incredibly naive, and I can't use her help at the camp."

Trevor's voice had grown clearer with each hurtful word, as if he and Sam were moving closer.

Isabel inched toward the bus.

Sam said something about Darla, but his quieter voice didn't carry over the sounds of the wind and the water.

"Right, but I doubt that she can handle camp cooking," Trevor responded, "and she'd surely get herself lost out in the back country."

"She'd be great with the kids, though." Sam sounded clear, as if he was very close. Slowly Isabel retreated toward the front of the lodge.

"That's your opinion," Trevor said. "Remember what happened with Betsy and Dylan? We're trying to get these boys to set loftier goals than their next hot date.

Half of them would get crushes on Isabel." He paused, then added in a lower voice, "I'm glad the camp boys didn't see the lingerie showing through her jacket a while ago."

Isabel's eyes flew down to her chest. Sure enough, she'd popped a button and her lacy bra was showing. That'd teach her to buy clothes off a department store rack without checking for good construction.

"I'm wondering if it's you who has the crush," Sam said, and he'd sounded as if he was a few feet away!

Whirling around, Isabel returned to the side entrance, hoping it was unlocked. It was, thank God. She escaped inside, then returned to the laundry room, where she found Angie still playing on the first token.

Isabel must have been gone five minutes, but she felt changed. And she'd learned something just now. Trevor certainly didn't have a crush on her. Despite what he'd told her, he had *problems* with her.

Personally.

Isabel bowed her shoulders and peeked down at her chest. The gap widened, forming a nice oval peephole that showed quite a bit of cleavage.

Lord. She'd wanted to look polished, that was all. She'd loved the outfit when she'd seen Peyton wearing it at the April wedding, and she'd been excited to find a copy at a Wichita store. She'd put the whole outfit, right down to the shoes, on her credit card.

She *never* used her credit card.

She reached down to tug the edges of the jacket together, then heard someone approach down the hallway. That wouldn't be Sam. He walked quietly, appearing in doorways as if by magic. This heavier step was Trevor's.

She let her hands fall to her sides and stepped farther into the room.

"I thought I heard that game going," he said from behind her. "Did you two find everything you need?"

He'd learned gracious behavior? Isabel turned, forcing herself to forget about whether her bra was showing. "We'll be fine."

"Sam said you might want a tour of the lodge?" he asked, his gaze moving downward. Now she knew why he'd been ogling her earlier. Then and there, Isabel decided she wouldn't allow him to intimidate her again.

She stood up straight and squared her shoulders. "No, thanks. We'll just hang out here until Darla arrives," she said, her voice syrupy.

He shrugged. "Suit yourself."

"Unless you have something for me to do now? Cook beans and wieners over a fire? Navigate an excursion across the Continental Divide?" She waited until she saw his forehead crease before adding, "Tempt a teenager?"

His eyes darkened. "You shouldn't have been listening."

"I didn't intend to listen," she said. "You should have been honest with me when I asked why you were so bothered. How can I be of any help to Darla and Sam if you're running around behind my back, telling them I'm worthless?"

Trevor blinked, gazing at her. "You're right," he murmured after a moment. "I should have talked to you about any problems."

Well, hallelujah! He hadn't apologized, but he'd admitted his mistake.

"You should also realize I didn't come here to be waited on," Isabel said. "I came to help Darla."

"I realize that."

She matched his stare until he turned around and left again. Then she stood for a moment, waiting for her knees to stop shaking.

She wasn't accustomed to confrontation. Not at all. But she couldn't allow the man to think he could walk all over her. She had too much Ella Blume in her, she supposed.

Isabel went to her room to change into shorts and a T-shirt, then spent the next hour playing the video game with Angie and trying like the dickens to forget Trevor Kincaid's words and actions.

When Darla arrived, Isabel's hug for her was long and enthusiastic. "It's so good to see you," she said as she backed away. "How's your mom?"

"Coping. She's awfully tired, but she keeps a good attitude." Darla frowned into Isabel's eyes. "And how are you, my dear? Sam said you and Trevor had a run-in?"

"After he knew who I was," Isabel said. "Please tell me he had an awful week. That his dog died or his girlfriend broke up with him or he forgot to pay some major bill."

"Sorry." Darla's hazel eyes were round with concern. "Trevor is generally levelheaded, but he can be intense about the summer camp. I'm sure he didn't mean to insult you."

Isabel rolled her eyes. "That's not what it sounded like to me. Who are Betsy and Dylan, anyway?"

Darla frowned. "He told you about them?"

"No, but he mentioned them as if they had something to do with my presence here."

Darla stepped into the hallway and motioned for Isabel to follow, then closed the door gently between them and Angie, still in the laundry room.

"Dylan was a camper," she said. "Sixteen, but grown-up good-looking and aware of it. Betsy was a twenty-two-year-old counselor Trevor hired for our first summer camp. She was cute and bubbly, and some of the guys had crushes on her. One afternoon when everyone was supposed to be out fishing, Trevor caught her in Dylan's tent."

"Having sex?" Isabel whispered.

"No, but almost. Trevor broke it up and lectured both of them." Darla shook her head. "That was all that happened, but the rumors flew and Trevor had to explain the situation to the parents. Now, he has a no-female-counselor policy for the camp. I help him, here and there, but I'm not blond or twenty-two."

Isabel was reminded of her mother's no-boys policy. "That explains quite a bit, actually, but most girls wouldn't dream of doing what Betsy did. Besides, I'm also older than twenty-two."

"Not by much." Darla grinned, looking Isabel up and down as if she was glad to see her. "And Trevor figures that even if the girls didn't do what Betsy did, the boys would imagine them doing it, and his vision for the camp would be undermined."

"His vision?"

"To teach the boys to make good choices for their futures."

"Oh. Well, that's admirable." Isabel opened the laundry room door again and stepped inside. "He could have explained that to me."

"He might talk to you more after he gets to know you," Darla said, remaining in the hallway. "For now, how about lunch?"

The game's constant beeps stopped, and Angie skipped to the doorway. "I'm hungry. Can I eat, too?"

"Certainly." Darla peered down at the little girl. "What sounds better? Ham sandwiches or peanut butter and jelly?"

"S'mores!"

Darla grimaced. "You want S'mores for lunch?"

"At R.J.'s sleep-away camp, he godda have S'mores," Angie said, licking her lips. "He said they godda have 'em every single day, wif a chocolate bar an' two marshmallows."

Darla laughed, promising to stock up on those ingredients as soon as possible.

She was still commenting on how cute Angie was an hour later, while she and Isabel stood at her kitchen sink washing lunch dishes. Angie was sitting nearby, devouring a slice of chocolate cake—the closest thing to S'mores that Darla had on hand.

Isabel and Angie spent the afternoon in the office with Darla, who was behind on paperwork. Isabel began addressing and stamping a stack of wedding invitations while Angie poked at the keys of an old manual typewriter.

The little girl wasn't a problem. Darla was clearly smitten with her, and the pair reminded Isabel of each other. Both were tiny, and both were full of bounce.

After dinner, Isabel took Angie to their shared bedroom so the little girl could talk to her dad and brother on the telephone. Isabel spoke to Roger only briefly, answering questions about her car's performance during the trip, then she handed the phone to the little girl while she sat nearby, stitching a beaded-bell wedding favor.

Angie prattled, telling her dad about their night in a Goodland, Kansas, motel, then she enumerated every detail about their arrival here—from the electronic game to the chocolate cake to the typewriter.

As she waited, Isabel thought about all that had happened today, too. However, she thought about the whole mess with Trevor Kincaid.

It was funny, but out there on the highway this morning, she'd felt playful and relaxed with him. Josie's flex-your-flirt-muscles advice had been fresh in her mind, so she'd been friendly to the good-looking stranger.

And when she'd touched him, she'd caught his reaction. His muscles had tightened, his eyes had erupted and her thoughts had turned shamelessly to what he must be like in bed.

The strength of her reaction to him had shocked her. She'd never felt such a surge of sexuality. Maybe she was a sexual adventurer at heart. Maybe that natural curiosity had caused her to be distracted. And maybe that was when Trevor had formed a bad impression of her.

Damn. She'd be a fool to worry about him. Her plan for the summer was to have a blast helping Darla while Roger stayed at home, hopefully missing her.

And she would have fun, she knew.

As soon as she stopped worrying about Trevor Kincaid.

Chapter Four

On Monday morning, Trevor parked in front of the lodge almost a full hour before his usual arrival time and sat eyeing the open door. That had to be Darla inside at this time of day. Darla made great coffee.

She usually didn't lecture, but Trevor had to admit, she'd been right to rough him up last Friday afternoon. He'd been a jerk. He hadn't meant to insult Darla's guests.

He'd meant to be strong. Brisk. Businesslike.

He'd overreacted to Isabel. But he'd be fine. After their embarrassing chat in the lodge laundry room, Isabel would surely keep him at a distance.

Which was best for all concerned.

When Trevor caught himself drumming on his steering column, replaying a few of last Friday's happenings, he yanked his keys from the ignition. After stepping out of his Jeep, he strode toward the entry and Darla's coffee.

He needed to catch up with work he should have done this weekend, when he'd stayed home to nurse his battle wounds. This morning, he'd round up the first-aid kits and get them out to the cabins before the counselors arrived for their initial day of training.

He walked into the main reception area, noted Darla's half-empty glass of iced tea on her coaster, then grabbed a cup of coffee and went through to his office.

Thankful for Darla's skill with the aging coffee machine, Trevor sat down to flip the pages of his desk calendar while he sipped. When he heard her shuffling papers at her desk a minute later, he called out a good morning.

She mumbled.

"Today's first-aid day," he said. "Can you help with the training after lunch? It'll probably take about two hours. The Walters boys ought to remember a lot from last year."

A silence followed.

Was she still upset about his bad behavior with her friend? But she'd already hollered at him for that. She should give him a chance to try again.

Trevor got up and walked to the doorway to check on her.

Isabel was sitting at Darla's desk, drinking iced tea from the same sort of glass Darla always used, pondering the same question he'd meant to ask Darla.

She appeared as stunned to see him in the doorway as he was to see her at Darla's desk. "First-aid day," she said. "Uh. Sure. Guess I could handle that."

What could he do? He'd promised everyone he would be a good sport and give Isabel a chance, and here she was indicating that she could help.

"Okay. Good. About one o'clock in the picnic area between the cabins."

"All right." She nodded, watching him, looking…expectant. She was waiting for him to leave.

He would, in a moment. Trevor raised his eyebrows and glanced around the reception area. "Where's your sidekick?"

"Which one?"

"Either."

"Now that the wedding is on again, Darla and Sam need to catch up on their premarital counseling sessions," she said. "They drove to Longmont to meet with the minister, and should return by lunchtime."

"And the little girl? Angie, was it?"

She didn't react to his recall of the child's name, even though Trevor was impressed with himself.

"She's asleep," Isabel said. "The housekeeper's over there making up the beds. She promised to call me the minute Angie wakes up."

Trevor had promised honesty. Now he'd see how Isabel reacted to it. "How will you handle her this afternoon?" he asked. "We'll be outside in a wooded area. She might be excited or whiny or afraid of bears. Will you be able to concentrate on the training?"

"She won't be there. Darla promised to take her swimming this afternoon."

So, Darla intended to babysit Angie at the pool, and Isabel planned to help him out at the cabins. That sounded backward.

"Or you could swim with Angie, and Darla could help me," he said, keeping his tone patient.

"I'm not a swimmer," she said. "I wouldn't be able to help Angie if she got into trouble."

"You don't swim at all?"

She shook her head, her blue eyes solemn. "Not at all."

Trevor frowned, again getting the vague impression that Isabel had stepped out of a simpler time. He wondered at the chances of her knowing first aid. Many of his counselors had learned basic first aid during swim lessons, and he built on that knowledge here at camp.

"All right, then. So you're Darla today?"

She managed a ghost of a grin. "Guess I am."

He glanced at his watch. "This year's counselors will begin arriving any minute. If you'll shoot them into my office, I'll get their paperwork finished."

Before Isabel could respond, the phone rang and she picked it up. "Burch Lodge, Isabel speaking."

Trevor waited, thinking he might need to take the call, but Isabel looked away from him. "Oh, good. Angie's awake. Be right over. Thanks."

So, Trevor was left to watch for his own counselors. He didn't see Isabel again until the afternoon, when his crew was gathering round the picnic area to start the first-aid training session.

This was a good bunch. The Walters brothers had worked at the camp last year. They'd been great with the younger boys and were talented climbers. The three new men, all college students, were enthusiastic and responsible.

Within a minute Isabel appeared down the narrow path that wound through a thicket of evergreens.

He watched his crew. Quick greetings were followed by long stares and big smiles.

Lord. He remembered what he'd been like at that age. Full of hormones, interested in almost any female and lacking a true concern for what might happen if a girl's yes led to a consequence.

For him it had. Eventually.

But Isabel had dressed conservatively, in khaki shorts much like his own. He'd just have to work harder to command the guys' attention. He indicated with a nod that Isabel should take a place at the tables, so she walked around to the front and sat down, ready to listen.

Atta girl. His best bet would be to just teach this thing, and maybe allow her to volunteer a wrist or an ankle for bandage wrapping.

He immediately began his talk, reviewing the procedures for shock and evacuation. When he started to talk about bleeding injuries, he was startled when Isabel stood up beside him to demonstrate the appropriate pressure points.

Minutes later, Isabel nodded when he talked about how to identify venomous spiders and snakes. When he described poison ivy and oak rashes, her raised hand surprised him again. "Yes, Isabel?"

"Calamine lotion works great, but you can also take vitamin C and calcium to prevent infection and boost your immune response."

Okay, she had some health knowledge. "Good. Thanks. Anyone else know alternative treatments?" Trevor glanced around at the college men.

Isabel shoved her hand in the air again.

"Yes?"

"You could mix water with oatmeal or cornstarch, making a paste to put on the rash, or you can even rub watermelon rind on it." She grinned at the guys, who'd chuckled at her sass.

"Watermelon rind?" he asked.

"It dries up the rash."

"Anything else?"

"If you break an arm or leg, go to the doctor."

Now the guys laughed out loud.

"And after she sets your bone, eat half a pineapple every day," she said. "Fresh pineapple, not canned. It contains an enzyme that reduces swelling."

Another obscure fact he hadn't known. Wonderful.

Trevor split the guys into pairs to practice CPR techniques, but his odd-numbered group left one man out.

"I'll work with someone," Isabel said.

Dusty, the one who'd been left without a partner, received a couple of claps on the back, but the guys weren't too obnoxious.

Judging from the twenty-year-old's reddening cheeks, he'd had more experience with campfires than females. "Don't get too happy," Trevor told him. "We're not actually performing CPR. No touching."

"Of course not, chief."

Trevor turned to address the group. "Walk each other though the procedures. I'll come round in a few minutes to check your techniques."

An hour later, they'd finished the course. After the counselors had demonstrated mastery of the necessary skills, Trevor thanked Isabel sincerely and watched her wander through the trees toward the lodge.

"What's up next, chief? We hiking this afternoon?"

Dusty's question interrupted thoughts Trevor didn't want to be having. He pulled his attention to his itinerary. "That's the plan," he said. "But you've earned a break. Grab your suits. We can take about an hour to swim."

The men scrambled into the cabins, but Dusty stayed behind. "Think we should invite Isabel to join us?" he asked.

That one was easy. "She doesn't swim."

Dusty stared at him a moment, his eyes huge behind his glasses. "We could ask her, anyway. She could stand around in the shallow end and cool off. She worked as hard as we did this afternoon, you know."

"I do know that, Dusty. But I don't think she'd be interested. Really."

Still, Dusty didn't leave. "Are you two, you know, dating?" he asked.

Trevor studied the younger man's intense expression. He was nerdier-looking than the average counselor, but he obviously had some guts.

He also had a good little crush going, damn it.

Trevor drifted toward the cabins, hoping Dusty would follow him as he awaited an answer.

He did.

They reached the doorway, and still Dusty waited.

Trevor pointed a thumb at the door. "Go get your suit, Dusty, and please remember why you're here. The kids arriving next week are at the age when they could head for trouble. They need strong male role models. That's you and me, okay? This isn't Find A Date.com."

Dusty vanished into the cabin. Finally.

But Trevor was still contemplating Dusty's question two evenings later, as he headed across to Sam and Darla's private dwelling for a barbecue.

He and his crew of big, sweaty guys had spent hours exploring trails, reviewing mountaineering safety and brushing up on their camp stove skills. They still had work to do before the campers arrived, but everyone was up for another break.

Trevor had given the crew a night of freedom, and they'd caravanned to Longmont to have dinner and visit the local pubs.

"Are you two dating?" Dusty had asked.

A simple question.

Should've been a simple answer: no.

But in refusing to answer it, Trevor had put a crazy idea into his own head.

Maybe he should relax.

Maybe he should allow himself to enjoy Isabel's company, and be sure the boys *noticed* him enjoying it.

The benefits would be several: Sam would stop hinting about wasted opportunities, and Dusty's tongue would return to his mouth. Perhaps Trevor would even figure out why he couldn't get Isabel out of his head.

Or maybe he should talk himself out of an idea that he'd normally find insane.

An evening in Isabel's company should help him answer the question, either way. One thing was for certain. The next few hours should be interesting.

He walked into the house through Sam's garage door, just as he always had, and found Sam and Darla talking in the kitchen while Darla pulled ingredients from the fridge. As soon as he walked in, they stopping chatting.

That was different.

Sam turned around on his stool to eye Trevor. "How was River Wall?" he asked, naming the crag where Trevor had taken the crew climbing this afternoon.

"Great. Dusty managed to get up Pocket Hercules, if you can believe that."

"Sure I can. The kid's tougher than he looks."

Trevor approached the breakfast bar and pulled out another stool, wondering about the whereabouts of Darla's house guests. But before he could sit, Darla caught his eye. "Hey, Trev, would you do me a favor?"

"Depends."

She nudged a platter of marinated chicken sitting on the center island. "The grill's already going. If you handle the entree, Sam here can help me finish the other dishes."

"Sam learn to cook sometime recently?"

"I've been teaching him a few things," Darla said, her hazel eyes narrowed. "He can set the table and round up drinks. You men are more resourceful than you look, you know."

"All right, all right! I'm going." Trevor walked across and grabbed the platter. "See you two later," he said, whistling on his way out.

Isabel would be outside, somewhere in the vicinity of the grill. Trevor didn't have to hear Sam and Darla's conversation to know what they'd plotted.

Not a setup—Darla and Sam weren't stupid—but a friendly meeting. They wanted their best friends to get along. Little did they know, Trevor *wanted* to see Isabel. He wanted to gauge their response to each other in a relaxed atmosphere and figure out for himself whether he should forget his crazy idea or go for it.

Sure enough, she was sitting in one of the Adirondack chairs, facing the tree-lined riverbank at the northwest edge of the property.

"You lose your buddy tonight?"

Isabel started, then jumped from her chair. "Oh, hi," she said, turning around to face him. "Angie's inside. She fell asleep a while ago."

He frowned as he opened the grill cover and began to transfer chicken pieces from the platter to the hot rack. "Before eight o'clock?"

"She's been avoiding naps. Maybe I should go check on her." Isabel approached him and the house beyond, her arms wrapped around her torso as if she was cold.

Trevor shifted toward her, blocking her path. "Please stay." At her surprised look, he explained, "I believe we've been sent out here on a mission."

She gazed at the now-empty platter. "To cook the meat course for our dinner?"

"No…well, yes. That, and getting to know each other better." He closed the grill cover, set the platter on the side table and peered at Isabel in the darkness. He wished he could see the expression in those deep blue eyes.

"Why?"

"I'm not sure, exactly. Probably because we're their

best man and maid of honor and they want their wedding to go well. And maybe also because we're their good friends, and they can't figure out why we didn't hit it off in the first place."

"Why didn't we?"

Of all the questions she might have asked, he hadn't expected that one. "Good question," he said, then strode across to the riverbank to grab two chairs and drag them closer to the grill. "It'll be warmer up here. Sit."

She sat alongside him and waited.

"Guess I'm pretty focused on the camp," he said, knowing he could only offer her a portion of the truth. The other explanation still confused him, and it might embarrass them both.

The unexplainable, inappropriate attraction.

"I come up here knowing it's a load of work and a big responsibility, and I guess I avoid possible problems."

"And you thought I'd be a problem because of what happened between Betsy and Dylan?"

"You know about them?"

"Darla filled me in."

"This camp means a lot to me," Trevor said. "I normally teach university students—environmental law— but these younger boys, well, there's a certain age when they can take the wrong path and wind up destroying their lives."

"Darla told me your vision for the camp," she said. "What you're doing is great."

Her opinion pleased him more than it should have. "Thanks," he said. He got up, lifted the grill lid and turned the meat, then returned to the chair beside her. "And I apologize for my earlier behavior. I overreacted to you, I think."

"But you realize now I'm no Betsy?"

He nodded. "Absolutely. And the counselors might notice your looks, but most of them know their boundaries."

She chuckled.

He gazed at her in the darkness. "What?"

"You said *most* of them. Guess you've noticed Dusty."

"How could I have missed Dusty?"

Isabel leaned toward Trevor. "He's come to the office at least four times a day, asking for things like extra backpacks and lanterns. Darla thinks he's stashing them under his bed or something."

"I didn't know about that. I'll keep an eye on him."

"Don't say anything to him," Isabel said, catching his hand momentarily. "I'm certain this is just an innocent…liking, for a person he admires."

"A young, attractive *woman* he admires," Trevor corrected. "I don't know how innocent it is, though. Guys that age have a lot going on in their heads."

"Oh, come on."

"Remember, I was that age once," he said. "Trust me. I know the kind of trouble those boys could face."

"You were some sort of juvenile delinquent?"

She wouldn't give up, would she? "No, but I was a bit of a…what's a genteel word? A rake. I was a rake. I'd have done more than just borrow a lantern."

"Even with an older woman?"

"Especially with an older woman, if she looked like you and she let me."

He knew he would see a blush on Isabel's cheeks, if not for the darkness.

"You're not that way anymore, are you?"

Sweet, small-town Isabel knew how to ask a direct question, didn't she?

"No. I'm not."

"What stopped you?"

Amused by her persistence, he got up to check the chicken and discovered it finished. He turned off the flame, then turned to glance at Isabel. "That's a tired story."

"Never mind, then. I'll just ask Darla later."

He laughed, then closed the grill lid and sat down. He'd get a clean platter in a moment, and carry the meat inside for dinner.

"I got into trouble when I was sixteen," he said. "A girl I'd known for about two weeks got pregnant."

Isabel remained silent. He could almost feel her willing him to go on. Surprisingly, he didn't feel reluctant to do so. "Clair—that was the girl—and I made plans to marry."

"After a two-week romance?"

"I wouldn't even call it a romance," he said, glancing into Isabel's face. "But, yes. Even though I didn't know her—I'd slept with her because I could— I wanted to give my child the Kincaid name and a stable home. I quit school and took a job as a night stockman. Clair and I got to know each other in infant-care classes."

"And then?"

Again, Trevor offered a palatable version of the truth. "And then, nature took care of our problem."

Trevor felt the soft touch of Isabel's hand on his. She moved it away and said, "I'm so sorry."

"It was a long time ago, and good things came out of it," he said. "Suddenly I was more interested in school than I'd ever been. I worked hard and finished my law degree early."

"And girls?"

"I took them more seriously. Waited until I knew them."

"That's a good thing."

"Sure, it is."

They might have talked more, but Darla walked outside with a clean platter. "You two okay out here? The meat's surely finished by now."

"We're fine, and the chicken's done." Trevor got up and stretched, then noticed that Isabel had stood up alongside him. An impulse to hug her and thank her for the talk stunned him.

Instead, he helped Darla transfer the meat to the new platter, then carried the old one and the spatula inside.

During the dinner conversation, Trevor learned that Isabel had grown up in a rural house, with two sisters and a single mother who had avoided public places and strangers.

Isabel had learned to cook at age eight and hadn't gone to a movie until she was seventeen, when her older sister's husband had sneaked her out. Except for her brother-in-law, she hadn't been around boys much at all. That might explain her curiosity about his past, and her patient affection for Dusty.

But the thing that stuck with Trevor most was that Isabel hadn't had an easy life, either.

If the troubles in his past had given Trevor a cynical heart, Isabel's past had left her entirely too trusting.

The sixteen-year-old Trevor wouldn't have known or cared that a woman as vulnerable as Isabel Blume existed. The grown-up Trevor was fascinated by her—a woman who was quite likely his opposite.

He was going ahead with his idea.

Chapter Five

On Saturday morning, Isabel ran the office again while Darla spent the morning helping Sam move cattle to their summer pasture. When Darla arrived, fresh from a shower after lunch, Isabel pointed to a classified ad in the newspaper. "Here's a DJ who claims to have more than a hundred wedding songs in his collection. Let's call him."

"Trevor hollered at me from across the porch," Darla said. "He needs help down at the cabins."

"This will take less than five minutes." Isabel hopped up from Darla's chair and handed her the phone receiver. "Then we can cross it off our to-do list."

"Trevor wants the help right now." Darla returned the receiver to its cradle.

Jeez. When the man said "jump," people jumped, didn't they? "That's fine, go on down," Isabel said. "But I can contact this DJ and get the information, if you'd like."

"No. Trevor wants you to come help him."

Isabel frowned. "Me."

Darla patted a stack of work on the corner of her desk. "He said he thought it'd be best if you helped, so I could get caught up on bookkeeping this afternoon."

Isabel kept frowning.

Darla sighed and shook her head. "All I can figure is that our dinner the other night was a wild success."

"What's he doing down there today, anyway?"

"The first-session camp kids arrive on Monday morning. He'll want to inventory the gear and mend any tents that need it."

Inventory and mending—those chores sounded do-able. Isabel looked down at Angie, who had been quite good all morning. She'd made some copies for Darla, then she'd clacked away at the old typewriter for a while. Now she was sitting on a bean bag chair they'd dragged in from the community room, thumbing through a stack of books. She had a jump rope waiting for when she got bored, which would probably be in about five minutes.

"What about Angie?" Isabel asked.

"Oh, leave her. She's content."

"Are you sure?"

"Absolutely," Darla said. "Believe me, Angie will liven up an otherwise boring afternoon."

"Do you mind staying here with Darla again, Ange?"

The little girl frowned. "What's inn-vinn-tory?"

"It's a way of counting things," Isabel said.

"I love to count!" Angie shoved her picture book off her lap and scrambled to her feet. "An' I can go way past twenty! Wanna hear? One, two, three…"

Isabel caught Darla's grin, as Angie continued. "That's great, hon," she said when the little girl stumbled after thirty-two. "But remember, I'm helping Trevor today. He'll need my attention, just like your brother does sometimes."

"Oh." Her bottom lip extended, Angie plopped down on the red vinyl chair. "Why are you helping that ol' Grinch, anyways?"

"You mean grouch?"

"Yeah. Why are you helping him?"

Isabel shrugged. "Because he asked me to."

"Make him ask someone else."

"I *want* to go." She did.

"Why?"

Isabel leaned down to Angie and spoke in a low voice. "Remember when you proved to R.J. that you could jump down from your daddy's tractor as easily as he could?"

"Yep. You said I ripped his socks off."

"I said you *knocked* his socks off," Isabel corrected. "And that's what I want to do, hon. I want to prove to Trevor that I can count as high as he can. I can do that better if you stay here with Darla."

Angie held her gaze for a moment, considering, then she said, "Okay. I can stay here an' watch *Shrek.*"

In the past week, the little girl had watched that movie twice a day, every day. "I brought other movies for you, hon."

"I like *Shrek.*"

"Sure, you can watch that one again," Darla interjected. "That donkey makes me laugh every time. I like him."

Isabel walked across to Sam and Darla's house to grab the *Shrek* DVD, then returned and popped it into the combination TV and player they'd set up in a corner of Darla's office.

After the movie started, Isabel wandered down to the kitchen. Whenever the lodge and cabins were fully booked, guests could choose to eat meals in the big dining hall or not. But during the camp weeks, Darla reserved the cabins and several of the lodge rooms for the kids and counselors.

Her part-time cook kept the refrigerator stocked with a variety of pick-up-and-go foods, and Darla encouraged everyone to act as if the big refrigerator were their own.

Isabel grabbed a couple of juice boxes, an apple and a package of cheese and crackers, hoping to save Darla a trip when the little girl asked for a snack.

With Angie settled, Isabel went to the lodge's communal bathroom to tidy her hair, then headed down to the cabins.

This afternoon should be interesting. She'd get a closer look at the attitude change she'd been noticing from a distance.

Thursday, she'd gone into Boulder with Darla and Angie. They'd checked out florists and bakeries and tried on attendants' dresses. Darla had also convinced Isabel to buy a swimsuit so she could at least stand in the pool with her and Angie.

That morning Isabel had said hello to Trevor and Sam from across the lodge porch before she'd gotten into the car to leave. Trevor had called out a greeting that could've melted butter.

Then, yesterday, he and the college guys had been gone all day, hiking and climbing somewhere. She hadn't seen them until late afternoon, when Trevor had waved at her from across the dining room. It'd been a wide wave. An enthusiastic one.

Apparently, their grill-side chat had made a huge difference in his opinion of her. Her polite-turned-surly highway rescuer had evolved to charmer.

But why? What did he want?

She was beginning to believe Trevor Kincaid was actually twins: one grumpy, one friendly.

Both confusing.

Isabel told herself it didn't matter. Her confidence had grown in the week she'd been here, and she was having the time of her life. Trevor might be intent on keeping her guessing, but her relationship with him could be a learning experience.

That was part of her reason for being here. Her sisters would certainly say so.

He was at the picnic tables again, shirtless this time, and with his back to Isabel as he spread out an extremely large, army-green tent and bent down to work the zipper.

Heavens, the guy had wide shoulders. She'd known he had a nice build, but who'd have figured that his clothes were hiding the sexiest male back she'd ever seen?

The play of muscles beneath smooth, tanned skin fascinated her. She called out a greeting through the scrub brush to warn him of her approach, but her tongue felt bulky. Her voice sounded thick. Had he heard her?

He turned around.

Whoa! Trevor's front was even better than his back. Slick with sweat, ridged with muscle and bone. Hard.

Lean.

Seriously sexy.

The corner of his mouth lifted, wooing her attention away from the span of muscles between his neck and belly button. "Isabel, there you are! I expected you a half hour ago. Come on around." He made a motion with his hand, as if to hurry her.

"I'm on my way," she said with a frown.

His smile was replaced by the row of forehead dimples. Trevor's expressions had certainly made an impression on her, hadn't they?

Isabel tried to recall Roger's smile. He sported a reddish-brown mustache and some light freckles on his cheeks, but what did his smile look like? His teeth were white and even, she remembered that. She couldn't remember his smile, though. Not at all.

Man, she was rattled.

Trevor grabbed a mustard-colored shirt from a nearby table and yanked it over his head. The gentlemanly action should have relieved some of Isabel's nervousness, but it didn't. Now that she had seen the body beneath, the thin, sweat-dampened material only made a nice frame for those muscles.

As Isabel entered the clearing, Trevor said, "Hey, I didn't mean to rush you. I was trying to be friendly."

"Huh?"

"You look perturbed."

Oh. Well, she was.

Isabel stopped a few feet away from him. "Where are the counselors?"

"Inside the cabins, readying the kids' bunks. They'll be carting blankets and sheets up to the lodge laundry room this afternoon."

"The cleaning staff doesn't do the cabins?"

"They could, but I think this is better for the crew. They'll be in charge of a group of younger boys in a couple of days, and they need to work well together. They do a lot of talking while those wash loads cycle through."

That made sense. "Want me to help them with laundry, then?" she asked, and wished she could un-ask the question as soon as it came out of her mouth.

He didn't want her to help the counselors.

He wanted her to help him.

For whatever, unfathomable reason.

"No, I want you to stay out here with me."

She'd known he was going to say that. And she could do this. She could be alone with Trevor among all these tall trees and bulging muscles. She could conquer this overpowering mixture of jumpiness and shyness and guilt, and do whatever Trevor needed her to do.

She *could.*

Isabel drew in a deep breath. Moving beyond him, she studied the miscellany of tents laid out on the tables.

"We're checking zippers? Should I start on these, over here?"

"Let's work together." He lifted a corner of the tent near him. "If you'll hold this up, I'll soap the zipper teeth."

She turned to him. "Soap the zippers?"

He grinned. "See? I know a few watermelon rind tricks, too. Soap keeps the zippers zipping, and it's afford-able."

They inspected each tent, checking seams and zippers and scraping rust from poles with sandpaper.

"Guess I never really grew up completely," Trevor said moments later as he stuck his finger through a ripped seam and tossed that tent into a pile to be repaired. "I still get excited about these backyard campouts with the boys."

Isabel studied the thick forest beyond the cabins. "Surely this won't be an ordinary backyard campout. How much land does Sam own, anyway?"

"Just over fifteen hundred acres," Trevor said. "The property extends about a mile beyond the trees on this side, but he has an easement into the Roosevelt National Forest. We do most of our hiking and climbing off-site."

At that moment, the five college men came out of the last cabin and hollered a greeting as they lugged several overfilled laundry baskets up the narrow path.

Intensely aware that she was alone in the woods with Trevor, Isabel refrained from asking any more ques-tions. Friendliness with a stranger on the highway had felt natural. Even their chat the other night had been all right.

But now she knew him better and liked him more, and that made all his attentiveness feel dangerous.

As they sat on either end of a shaded bench to stitch torn seams and mesh inserts, a woodpecker tapped on a distant tree. A breeze lifted Isabel's hair, cooling her face and making the warm day pleasant. The woodsy smells of thick plant life and raw, warming earth filled her senses.

She began to relax.

"You said at dinner the other night that you are close to your sisters," Trevor said. "Tell me about them."

Isabel sensed that he'd stopped working to look at her, but she kept her eyes on her needle and thread. "I told you about my big sister, right?"

"Some. Tell me more."

Isabel pushed the sturdy needle through the heavy canvas, then pulled it out. "She and Ethan have a two-year-old boy, and Callie does cancer research for a Wichita hospital."

"Must be smart."

Isabel smiled to herself. She and her sisters each had special gifts, their mother had taken pains to tell them often, but one of Callie's greatest was certainly her intelligence.

"I suppose you'd say Callie's the brainy one."

"And your other sister?"

"Josie's a couple years younger than me and works as an interior designer." Isabel thought about her baby sister, who had scads of male friends and not a shy bone in her body. "She's the gregarious one."

"You must be the beautiful one, then."

She glanced across at him, and he moved his gaze slowly down to her mouth and back up.

What was he *doing?*

"Oh, no," Isabel said. "I'm not the beautiful one. I'm the homebody. I like family and quiet things."

Her mother had always said so.

Trevor raised his brows. "The type who would bring the neighbor's kid along on a summer trip, for instance?"

Did he have to bring that up again? Angie had been a sweetheart, but Darla and Isabel were constantly trading off chores and child-care duties.

Although Sam and Darla currently had a few other adult guests staying at the lodge, Darla had altered the menus to suit a little girl's tastes. Right now she was doing her office work to the sounds of *Shrek*.

Darla said she enjoyed it, but the extra distractions and responsibilities couldn't help.

Isabel sighed. "That's right. Listen, I might occasionally let my good intentions get in the way of my judgment, but this arrangement will be fine, too, I promise. Angie will be going home soon."

"I was teasing." Trevor held her gaze.

Lord, those eyes were sexy.

And if Isabel didn't know better, she'd think the man was trying to...*woo* her.

But...why?

"Angie hasn't been a problem so far," he said.

"Not a problem?" she repeated, scowling as she returned to her work. Or tried to.

"Not really."

Before she yanked the needle right through her flesh, Isabel stopped sewing and let the torn corner of the tent fall to the ground. Then she met his stare and held it.

"What are you doing, Trevor?"

"What do you mean?"

"Do you have a twin or a look-alike cousin?"

"No."

"Then you must be messing with my head." She shrugged, frowning. "First you're polite. That I understood because we were strangers on the highway. But after you learned who I was, you were cross. Rude, even. A week later and you're full of compliments?"

He peered out at the thickness of trees for a moment, then nodded. "I know I'm sending mixed signals," he said, his voice low and personal. "On the highway I was charmed by a beautiful stranger, but one I didn't think I'd ever see again. Polite behavior fit the situation."

She felt herself blush. "And when I showed up here?"

"I was still charmed."

"You were not!"

"Yes, I was. But I had a lot to do and worried that you'd be a distraction," he said. "I was probably searching for reasons to dislike you."

"And now?"

"Now I'm realizing it can't hurt to get to know you. We had a nice talk before dinner the other night." He held her gaze for an impossibly long time.

Green. She'd just figured it out. Trevor's eyes were a sexy, grayish green.

Isabel broke their stare and frowned down at her stitching again. She stabbed the needle into the cloth. Yanked it out. Fretted.

He wanted to get to know her, how?

And she wished she knew what he'd meant by *charmed.*

Anyone could be charmed by a person they'd recently met who was intriguing or cute or full of personality.

Or did Trevor mean charmed as in attracted to her, specifically?

Damn, she'd just pricked her thumb. She slowed her movements, sighing. Thinking.

Surely, Trevor wasn't suggesting that they engage in a summertime fling? She had Angie to worry about. And hadn't she mentioned Roger, back home in Kansas?

No. She hadn't. When the subject of Angie's identity had come up, she'd claimed that Angie's father was a neighbor. Not a boyfriend and certainly not a possible future husband.

She sighed again and kept sewing, thinking it was a good thing she was working with a tent. Her stitching was awful. Uneven, loose.

Trevor hadn't been the only one charmed by a stranger out there on that highway. She should tell him about Roger, here and now.

And she would have, if not for the technicality that she wasn't dating Roger, here and now.

She should tell Trevor that she wasn't the type to engage in a summertime romance. They could get past this tension-filled moment and direct their attention elsewhere. Except, well, dammit, she didn't know if he was suggesting a summertime romance.

Besides, she'd had thoughts of kissing him. *Maybe she was the fling type after all.* As Josie would say, how would she know unless she exercised those flirt muscles?

She glanced his way and discovered him still watching her. "Okay. Well, thanks for explaining," she said, sounding and feeling lame.

"What did you think I was doing?" he asked.

The question startled her. She put needle to cloth again, avoiding his gaze. "Lord, I don't know," she said. "I thought maybe Darla had clobbered you, after that first day."

"She did."

Isabel peered at him and laughed.

"She threatened to, anyway," he said. "I hadn't realized I was being such a chump."

Again, Isabel had no idea what to say, so she resumed her sewing while Trevor folded the other tents and carried them into a cabin.

When Isabel finished, she carried the last tent into the same cabin, and at his direction slid it onto a shelf inside the entryway. Then she helped him count lanterns, sleeping bags and camp dishes.

With each tick she made on the printed inventory sheet, Trevor smiled or made a joke or brushed a hand against her hand or arm or leg.

Then, he walked her to the lodge and said another warm goodbye before he disappeared into the laundry room, at the opposite end of the building from Darla's office.

Isabel found Darla and Angie outside on the porch. The little girl was jumping rope while Darla sat in a rocker nearby, punching numbers into a calculator and scribbling the results into a book that she'd opened over her lap.

"Hi, Izza-bell," Angie said, speaking in time to her jumps.

"Hi, Ange. Did you finish your movie?"

"Yep. Did you finish helping the grinch?"

Isabel put her finger to her lips. "Yes, I did," she said. "But please don't call him that anymore, hon."

"Okay. That grouchy-face."

Isabel shook her head. "Not that either."

Angie landed flat on her feet and stood gaping at Isabel while the rope slapped down hard against the concrete porch. "Why not?"

"Because he's trying to be friendly now, I guess. And because everyone deserves a second chance."

"Oh." Angie started skipping rope again. "What should I call him, then?" she asked. "Professor?"

"No one up here calls him by his title. Maybe you could call him Mr. Kincaid or perhaps Mr. Trevor. Or Professor. Next time we see him, we can ask which he'd prefer."

"Okay." The little girl began to chant a counting rhyme, effectively ending the conversation.

"Things went okay, then?" Darla asked, glancing up.

"They did." Isabel claimed the chair next to Darla. "If your little talk had this much effect on Trevor, I'm impressed."

"Oh, but he's usually friendly enough," Darla said. "I think he probably just needed to get to know you. For some reason, your chance meeting on that highway threw him off." Her gaze drifted down to her numbers, and she become immersed in them again.

Darla was right. Trevor had been friendly this afternoon. Not overly attentive. He'd confessed that he was charmed by her, but he hadn't suggested a torrid affair.

Not at all.

Isabel watched Angie play and chastised herself for being so silly. Trevor had only been making amends this afternoon—not moves. A more experienced woman would have recognized that. She'd be foolish to give the idea another thought.

Or his muscled torso, with the shirt or without it.

Lord. Those ripples had been perfect. They'd made her wonder what it would feel like to touch them. His skin would be hot and firm and—

"Hey, Izza-bell!" Angie paused in her rhyme but continued to jump. "Did you rip his socks off?"

The shedded clothes in Isabel's mind were definitely not socks. "Huh?"

"The grinch!" Angie said in a stage whisper. "Did you teach him you can count higher than him?"

"Oh. You mean, did I knock Mr. Kincaid's socks off."

Isabel watched Darla's hand still over her bookkeeping.

Obviously, she was interested in this answer, too.

"Maybe in a way," she said, realizing as she spoke that it had been the other way around.

If anyone's socks had been knocked off this afternoon, they were hers. Trevor had needed only to offer normal friendliness and a glimpse of his tanned flesh, and she'd been swayed.

Developing a crush on a complicated man like Trevor Kincaid would be a mistake. Whether they were on a break or not, Isabel shouldn't give up on Roger.

He might be reluctant to marry a second time, but she thought he'd eventually settle down again.

And that was what she wanted, wasn't it? Marriage to a man who would stick around. And happy children. She thought she could achieve that with Roger. If she counted Angie and R.J., she was halfway there.

Darla had told her recently that Trevor was thirty-two. Actually, he was a year older than Roger, and he'd never been married. Isabel thought it was safe to assume that he didn't have kids. He was a committed bachelor, she had no doubt, and she could see why.

An enigmatic, sexy man like Trevor could very well die a bachelor.

Chapter Six

Three hours later, Isabel sat dangling her feet in the pool while Darla taught Angie to float at the opposite end. With Sam's cell phone pressed to her ear, Isabel listened as Roger told her that he was surprised his son could be so much help around the farm.

She felt for a moment as if she was at home in her own kitchen, checking in with Roger after his workday. "And how is R.J.?" she asked. "Is he enjoying Angie's absence as much as he thought he would?"

"So far."

Isabel heard a click and a whir, and knew her ex-boyfriend and possible future husband was putting bacon in the microwave, cooking it for his standard Friday night dinner. She also knew that, without prompting, Roger wouldn't elaborate much about R.J.'s well-being. The only son of a reticent farmer whose wife had died young, Roger had never been a talker.

That was another reason he and Isabel got along so well. In a world where people couldn't drive their cars or go to a movie without feeling a need to talk on the phone, they both understood how to be alone.

Another sound, and Isabel knew Roger was opening the utensil drawer, grabbing his good utility knife to slice a couple of tomatoes. He'd make four sandwiches, cutting each one corner to corner and putting the resulting triangles on paper plates, corners inward so the sandwiches would fit. He and his son would eat with the kitchen television tuned to the Weather Channel.

"What else has been happening?" Isabel asked.

"Oh, you know. R.J. hops between his computer games and the TV. He's trying to top a buddy's high score on some game. Snicker? Snooker?"

"Snood. He plays Snood."

"Oh." Roger paused, then said, "Iz, are you ready to come home, yet?"

Could he already miss her, Isabel wondered. "Darla's wedding is on the third Saturday in July. I'm here until then," she said.

"There's a dance out in Leon later this month." Roger said this as if it was big news, but for the past five or six years, folks from the town about ten miles east of Augusta had held that same, monthly dance.

Maybe he did miss her. "I know about the Leon dances," she reminded him. "You used to take me."

"You don't want to go this month? I can get tickets."

"I can't, Roger. I'm here."

He was quiet, and Isabel felt guilty, and she had an idea. Roger's wife had been his high school sweetheart, so he'd been involved with only two women—Isabel and Barbara.

Maybe he should check out the competition this summer, too. He'd either learn to appreciate Isabel or he'd become interested in someone else.

It was a risk, but a real breakup would be better than this sort-of-dating-but-sort-of-bored status they'd been stuck in.

"Maybe you should ask someone else," she said.

"Someone else?"

"We're taking a break, remember? That leaves you free to take someone else to the dance."

"You'd want me to do that, Iz?"

Lord, she didn't know. Somehow, she didn't think she'd mind that much if it'd drive their relationship forward.

"I'd understand if you did."

A flash of tanned skin caught Isabel's eye, and she glanced up in time to watch Trevor streak across the space at the opposite end of the pool. He entered the water with a tidy splash and traversed the space in a straight line that would end where Isabel was sitting.

She lifted her feet from the water, crossing them beneath her. As she watched those strong arms propel across the water, she tried to concentrate on Roger's voice.

Even though she'd just told her boyfriend to date someone else, she was noticing Trevor.

She closed her eyes to make focusing easier.

Roger seemed to be suggesting that they attend *next* month's dance. Before she could comment, she heard a splash at her feet. She opened her eyes to see Trevor's head emerge through the water's surface right in front of her. He dragged a hand across his eyes, flinging water droplets onto her legs. Then he grinned at her.

She held the phone out to indicate that she was busy,

so he nodded and swam away. For several more minutes Isabel continued talking to Roger. Sort of.

She listened. She responded in the appropriate places. But Trevor's antics in the pool held her attention. Finally she made excuses to hang up and got up to set the phone on a stack of dry towels on the chaise longue behind her.

When she'd returned to her place at the side of the pool, Trevor appeared in front of her again. He gripped the pool ledge very near her thigh, and looked up at her. His hand and face—his entire person—was close enough to make Isabel wish she could run into the lodge and escape this overwhelming mixture of confusing feelings.

Maybe her older sister, Callie, had been right. Maybe she should have used this vacation to stay away from men entirely. Get her head straight.

"Angie said you were talking to her dad," Trevor said.

Great. He'd mentioned Roger and presented an opportunity for Isabel to tell the truth about that relationship. Trevor had been honest with her about things and deserved the same from her.

"Yes, I was," she said.

"I presume all is well in Augusta, Kansas?"

All was the same in Augusta, it seemed. Isabel figured she hadn't been away long enough to miss it as much as she'd thought she would. "Sure. Things are fine."

She frowned at Trevor, wondering why being wet would make him look so different. She'd never thought of him as handsome, exactly—not in the way Roger was handsome—but something about Trevor's looks turned her stomach to jelly.

That had never happened with Roger.

Trevor was bigger in her thoughts, somehow. His very life seemed bigger. But Isabel wasn't sure she was being fair to Roger. She watched Trevor's gaze move down her pale-pink swimsuit. The one-piece covered more skin than any of the other suits she'd found in the Boulder shops, but it hugged her curves. She felt exposed.

And tense and guilty and excited.

Trevor flattened his palms on the concrete beside her, then pulled his body out of the water, flipping around at the same time so she caught a glimpse of his wet, muscled backside before he sat down.

Jeez. She could actually hear her heart pounding. Perhaps it was time to head inside. Angie and Darla had been out here an hour and should be quitting soon.

"Do you have something against swimming?" he asked, eyeing the dry, flimsy material of her suit again in a way that wasn't at all gentlemanly.

She had thought about jumping into the shallow end with Darla and Angie. Playing in the pool sounded like fun. Now that she had a suit, nothing was stopping her.

Except for the thought of Trevor being in there with her. With her luck Angie and Darla would leave and she'd be alone with him, trying to convince herself that he wasn't making moves on her, even though a part of her wanted him to be making big moves on her.

Big. Bold. Unmistakable. Unforgettable. Moves.

If he wasn't flirting, then why had he sat down there beside her? Why was he ogling her like that? And why on earth was he leaning so close that she could feel his body heat?

"Where are the counselors?" she asked.

His intent look sent a spasm of erotic heat straight down her center. "They're gone."

She frowned.

"I always give the counselors twenty-four hours off before the camp kids arrive," he explained. "That means I get twenty-four hours off, too, to do whatever I want."

Had he just waggled his brows at her?

"Oh. That's nice."

God. What an inane comment!

Isabel felt like a boring, inexperienced woman who couldn't even tell if a man was attracted to her. If she stayed a moment longer, Trevor would surely discover that that was exactly who she was.

Not a temptress at all.

Lord help her, she'd rather be a temptress.

Once again, she thought about getting up to leave, but Trevor chose that moment to slip into the pool. Instead of swimming away, however, he treaded water in front of her. "Come on in," he said.

"What?"

"I'll be right here with you." He glanced at Darla and Angie, mere yards away. "I can teach you to swim while Darla works with your sidekick."

"Trevor, she's a little girl. I'm a grown woman."

His raised eyebrows told her he'd noticed.

The man was coming on to her. Definitely.

"Don't you think it's time you learned?" he asked. "You don't seem to be afraid of the water."

"I'm not."

"What do you have to lose?"

Her dignity.

Her composure.

Her very life, if she jumped in, landed on top of the guy and knocked both of them out. "I don't know."

His hands and eyes summoned. "Come on. I won't bite."

Not even a nibble?

That was Isabel's immediate thought, and she couldn't believe it. Lust controlled her brain right now. If her mother was watching from the other side, she must be shocked.

Hey! She would be shocked, wouldn't she? Ella Blume wouldn't have listened to this guy for a minute. She'd have headed inside a long time ago.

And Isabel, who worried every day that she was too much like her mother, decided to be different.

Immediately, she got up and stood with her toes poised over the edge of the pool. Trevor reached his hands out, as if he expected her to jump straight into his embrace. But she couldn't go that far.

"I'll walk over to the steps," she said, indicating with a sideways nod that she was heading for the shallow end.

He started in that direction underwater while she took off on foot. When she descended the concrete steps at the end, Angie shrieked. "Izza-bell! Are you getting in the pool, too?"

Pulling her gaze from Trevor's swimming form, Isabel nodded at Angie and Darla. "I am."

"Hip, hip, hooray!" The little girl, who'd been practicing head bobs, splashed her way over, arriving at Isabel's side at the same time Trevor did. "Is Mr. Trebor teaching you?" Angie asked in a stage whisper.

"Guess so."

"It's easy," Angie said. "He'll hold you and you can float on top of the water. Watch me!"

Darla came over to help the little girl show off her new skills, and with each maneuver Isabel imagined Trevor's hands touching her tummy and back, wherever Darla's hands touched Angie.

Strange. The water did little to cool Isabel's warming limbs.

After a while Darla told Angie that she wanted her to practice kicking before they quit for the day, so the two of them returned to the edge of the pool.

"You ready?" Trevor asked. "As Angie says, it's easy. I'll put my hand here." He spread his palms around her waist. "Relax backward. I'll hold you."

It was becoming clearer and clearer to Isabel that Trevor hadn't meant to say that she was charming *in general*.

When he laughed, he watched her mouth as if he wanted to coax a chuckle from it. When his glance captured hers, and it did often, he allowed his gaze to linger. Even now, he stood a little too close and allowed his hands to move a little too lovingly against her skin.

This swim lesson couldn't have anything to do with relaxing.

But Isabel managed to lie back, allowing her legs to drift up. Allowing her eyes to meet his.

"Beautiful," he said, his tone suggesting that he wasn't speaking about her float.

She should tell him that she expected to have a future with Roger when she returned home.

As if she felt guilty.

Trevor yanked his hand out from beneath her. If she was involved with Angie's father, then what was she doing here in this pool with him?

Well, drowning, for one thing.

Instead of getting her feet beneath her, she'd sunk.

Good God! Trevor thrust his hands in the water, gripping Isabel's upper arms and pulling her to her feet. Then he hauled her into his arms and carried her into the shallower water.

After she'd stood up and sputtered the water from her mouth, she glared at him. "You dropped me!"

Trevor let go of her again. "I know."

She reached up to swipe a curtain of wet, dripping hair out of her face. Then she glanced toward Darla and Angie, apparently making sure they were otherwise occupied. Finally she asked, "On purpose?"

"Didn't you hear? Angie announced your secret."

She rolled those pretty eyes, then shook her head. "What secret?"

He made an educated guess. "That her dad is your lover."

She stared at him. "I'm a small-town, girl, Trevor. I don't have a lover."

"Your boyfriend, then. She implied that her dad is your boyfriend."

"No. I believe she said that her father misses me," she said. "Since his ex-wife and I are both gone, Roger is in charge of his son. He isn't used to the responsibility on a full-time basis."

"You watch your neighbor's kids so much that their own father isn't accustomed to having them around?"

She blinked water droplets from her eyelashes. "Yes."

"Why?"

That got her. She blinked more but said nothing.

"Angie said you'll be her evil stepmother," Trevor said. "I couldn't have mistaken that."

"Oh, for God's sake. Angie wants me to be her step-mom. Roger and I have dated, but we're not together now, okay? Don't you have ex-girlfriends?"

He shrugged. "A few."

"You haven't told me about them."

Of course he hadn't. His exes were long gone. He didn't talk to them on the phone, and he most certainly didn't cart their kids across state lines.

"What's the problem, anyway?" she said. "I don't see why Angie's announcement would make you drop me like a hot potato."

Like a hot *something*. Not a potato.

Trevor took in the picture of Isabel, standing belly-deep in the water wearing a swimsuit that would be considered conservative. Except that from a distance, the color looked a lot like flesh. A person could form the impression she was naked and sexy as hell. If that weren't enough, he might also like the way she listened and asked good questions. He might begin to think some part of his feelings were real.

He might feel duped.

"Because we were flirting," he said. "Or so I thought."

She frowned at him, then glanced at Darla and Angie. So did Trevor. Darla was talking to the little girl nonstop, probably trying to keep her attention diverted.

Isabel started toward the pool steps. "We should go somewhere else to discuss this."

She was right. This wasn't the time or place to talk about what the two of them were or were not doing together. The little girl who might or might not be Isabel's future stepkid was right there, next to spitfire Darla.

No need to get anyone's hackles up.

"I'll follow you in a minute," he hollered after Isabel.

She kept sloshing her way to the steps and didn't acknowledge his declaration.

That was a good thing, because Trevor didn't want to explain his lack of haste. He fell into the water and started a backstroke to the deep end. There, he paused long enough to notice Isabel disappear inside the lodge, then he flipped to his belly and began a punishing front crawl.

After a couple of laps, he'd managed to subdue the arousal he'd been battling for a little while now.

Ever since he'd imagined Isabel naked.

He pulled himself out at the steps and followed her wet tracks to the lounge chairs, where he grabbed a towel. On his way inside, he dried himself off and wrapped the thick cloth around his hips. Just in case.

She was standing in the community room, adjusting a towel around her bottom in the same way he had. When he approached, she looked up and frowned at him. "So. You were flirting with me."

Trevor moved his gaze across her flushed cheeks, then down to her chest and up to her questioning eyes.

Had he misread the cues?

"I thought we were both flirting." Hadn't he explained that before?

As if she'd suddenly become aware of her barely concealed breasts, Isabel crossed her arms in front of her. But her nipples had been pebbled every time he'd looked. Outside, he might have blamed it on cool air against wet skin. But the lodge was warm. Stuffy, even.

Oh, yeah. She was attracted to him. He'd bank on it.

"You don't even like me," she announced.

"Huh?"

"You told Sam you didn't want me around, remember?" she said. "Did my knowledge of natural health cures really convince you I was flirt-worthy?"

Trevor had barely had time to consider a rebuttal before she continued, "And don't tell me you're charmed by me. Something else changed your behavior. What was it?"

They'd talked about this before, too. Was Isabel trying to divert his attention?

Possibly.

Probably. But he wasn't biting. Right now, they were discussing her involvement with Angie's father.

Right now, Trevor was kicking himself. He'd dropped Isabel because he'd been surprised and hurt. Also, he was a mite stunned that he was surprised and hurt.

Damn it. He'd opened his emotions to her.

"Did Roger do something awful?" he asked. "Sleep with someone else?"

"What? No." She looked horrified.

"Did you two just break up?"

She bit her lip, and he knew.

She'd broken things off with Roger very recently.

Trevor was her rebound guy.

Wow. He'd never been a rebound guy.

This was…embarrassing. The thing to do now was to back off and head home.

"Trevor, I'll be honest with you," Isabel said. "Roger and I did break up right before I came out here. We've dated three years, and I learned recently that our relationship was going nowhere. I don't know what will happen in the future. Does it help to know that?"

He studied her. Her brows were raised, her eyes wide, her lips relaxed. She'd offered him the truth, and in doing so had returned some of his dignity.

"Sure, it does," he said.

"Now will *you* be honest with *me?*"

He thought he had been. He'd tried.

"Are you starting a friendship with me, or are you thinking about more?"

If he wanted an out, she'd just offered him one. He could tell her he'd been trying to be friendly, not amorous. That he was sorry to have confused her, but no offense, and he'd try harder not to act smitten when he really wasn't.

He didn't want an out. Not yet.

He'd only deny his attraction to save himself from embarrassment—which was not a respectable reason. Besides, he still had the hormone-charged camp kids to worry about.

Or maybe he was just fooling himself.

Something about Isabel had snagged his full attention, and he wanted to know her. Sam had been right all along. He had a crush. He wasn't fifteen, though, and right now, he couldn't be more glad.

He smiled at Isabel. "Confession time," Trevor said. He took Isabel's arm to guide her farther into the lodge. "Have a seat."

"My suit is wet."

"Relax, the furniture in here is sturdy," he said. "Remember, Sam equipped this place to handle heavy use by sweaty, bug-sprayed guests and campers."

She eased into a wicker love seat and pulled a flower-shaped pillow over her middle.

He claimed the chair across from her and leaned forward. "Are you sure you're not currently involved with Angie's dad?"

She sighed. "I told him today I thought he should date other people. I'm trying to think about other things."

"Are you okay with the breakup?"

"I've been so busy I haven't thought about it much."

Trevor leaned forward and put his hand over Isabel's towel-covered knee. "You surprised me, you know. That's why I dropped you in the pool."

She nodded.

Funny, how well the truth worked.

"I thought I could ignore my attraction to you. Obviously, I'm liking you more than I'd expected. I'm sorry if I haven't made myself clear."

Her eyes dropped to his hand, still on her knee.

Without thinking about it, he moved it away, respecting her boundaries.

"I'm sorry I didn't tell you about Roger," she murmured.

He slid a hand down her upper arm and could feel her goose bumps.

She liked his touch, he assumed.

He looked into her eyes. "So if you're not involved with him now, things are okay between us."

"I guess so," she said, her eyes confused.

He might have backed away then, allowing both of them time and space to recover from a turbulent afternoon.

But she stared at his chest, and he felt more inclined to puff it out than cover it up. She looked up into his eyes, then let her attention drift down to his lips.

And linger.

He leaned forward and claimed her mouth.

Hadn't she been asking for a kiss with that look?

Then why was she keeping her mouth so stiff?

Trevor frowned, thinking she was going to pull away and tell him he'd misread cues again.

But she remained there, her lips against his. Willing, but perhaps not completely certain about what was happening. Her lips remained firm even after he inched in closer and tried again.

Hell, she was probably still thinking about Roger.

Trevor couldn't let her get away with that. She was with him now. He'd wanted to knock any thoughts of another guy clean out of her head.

Trevor scooted forward off his chair, resting his hands lightly on Isabel's arms and pressing his face closer to hers. He angled his jaw and nibbled teasingly against her lips.

No go.

She kept her mouth closed as if she were a twelve-year-old girl who was kissing a boy for the very first time.

That was when Trevor really put himself into the task. He firmed his grip on her, moving forward on his knees until they were chest to breast. Tummy to belly.

Arousal to seat cushion.

He retreated a half inch, then moved his hands to her hips. He softened his mouth, slanted it in the other direction, opened it to capture her, then ran his tongue along her bottom lip.

She made a mewling sound against his mouth. Then she opened herself up to him.

She was sweet. Soft. Sexy.

Trevor stayed there for a moment, teasing with his lips and tongue while her murmurs made him want to crawl into the love seat with her. She became bolder then, touching the tip of her tongue to his. Her hands gripped his bare shoulders, then skimmed his bare chest.

She was into his kiss now. Enjoying it fully, and getting better and more passionate with each passing second. Almost as if she was *learning* to kiss.

Could her earlier hesitation have been born of inexperience rather than indecision?

No. She was way past twelve, and she'd dated Roger for three years, she'd said. She'd been battling old loyalties, surely.

But Trevor opened his eyes and saw the dazed expression in those blue depths, and realized he might be encouraging a newly emerging sexuality in her.

The thought sent him reeling, and he was breathing hard and wishing he could make the other choice. That he could peel off all the wet towels and go for it.

Isabel was either loyal to a man who may or may not deserve it, or she'd had a very limited sex life. Trevor didn't know which was the case, but he'd have to be careful not to feel too challenged by the question.

She might be Sleeping Beauty, but he didn't feel like any Prince.

He still couldn't believe in the fairy tale.

Chapter Seven

The first group of boys arrived by bus on Monday morning, and Isabel soon recognized exactly how much extra work they created at the camp. She helped Darla in the office most of the time, but even that was chaotic. Kids interrupted constantly to deliver messages, drop mail in the outgoing slot or ask if anyone had turned in their lost eyeglasses or flashlights or socks.

This group, who ranged in age from twelve to fifteen, would spend the first few days learning to pitch tents and load backpacks, also taking longer and longer day excursions in preparation for some overnight trips they'd tackle later in their program.

Isabel saw Trevor only once that week. On Thursday he poked his head inside the main office to inquire about an absent camper. After Darla's explanation that the kid had developed a nasty case of chicken pox and gone home, Trevor turned his gaze to Isabel, offering a quick wink before he left.

Roger wasn't a winker, so that wink had been Isabel's first from a man. It had felt like a silent, secret hello, and it had left her glowing for most of the day.

Well. That wink, and memories of his kiss.

She wanted to try another.

But of course, Trevor was busy with the camp, and Angie had started to grow bored with the office routine. Isabel worked harder to entertain her and wondered how things might change after Barbara collected Angie in a couple of days.

If Trevor had free time between sessions, she'd be available. What would happen between them?

The next morning Isabel was alone in the office when the phone rang. She finished tightening the string on the last of her beaded-bell favors, then grabbed it. "Burch Lodge, Isabel speaking."

"Hello, Iz."

It was Roger.

Isabel closed her eyes, summoning an image of Roger's face. "Hi. How are things in Kansas?" she asked.

"Barbara's home," he said, speaking of his ex-wife. "Her new husband booked a return flight through the Wichita airport."

Barbara was supposed to have flown through Denver, to pick up Angie there. "How will Angie get home?"

"That's why I'm calling," he said, sighing. "The newlyweds have decided to move to Texas. Barbara's new husband has family there."

"Oh, no!"

"Oh, yes," Roger said. "They're going to pack more

clothes and go house and job hunting. Barbara's informed me that I should keep the kids until she gets settled."

Isabel's heart sank.

"I hate to ask, but could you keep Angie there until I find a way to get her?"

She'd known he was going to say that. "How are you going to find time to come?" she asked. "It's a day's drive each way."

"I know."

Damn it. Isabel glanced out the office door, to where Angie was skipping rope on the porch.

She didn't deserve to be treated as if she were a problem. She wasn't a problem. Isabel had simply been excited at the thought of spending time alone in Colorado—her first independent vacation as an adult woman.

"So what are you going to do?" Isabel asked.

"Would you mind keeping her? Or, I could have my aunt watch her. But I don't like making Angie go over there."

She hoped not. The woman had a paddle hanging on a peg in her kitchen, and she hadn't heard modern-day warnings against corporal punishment. Once, she'd paddled R.J. for leaving the peanut butter jar open.

Perhaps this was fate, preventing Isabel from flirting where she shouldn't.

"As far as I'm concerned, Angie can stay," Isabel said. "But I'll have to run the idea by Darla. I'll call you."

After talking with Roger for another minute, Isabel

hung up and sat staring at the phone, trying to talk herself out of a bad mood. Here she was again, changing her plans to mesh with what everyone else wanted and needed.

But she wouldn't send Angie to her great-aunt's paddle, just so she could indulge in a romance that would eventually lead nowhere.

Trevor lived in Colorado. She lived in Kansas.

She wanted marriage. Kids. A certain future.

Roger had kids she already loved. Perhaps she could give him kissing lessons.

When the phone rang again, she picked it up and forgot she was answering the Burch Lodge phone. "H'lo?"

"Isabel?"

This was Trevor. She felt her tummy flip. "Yes?"

"I ran into a snag out here and could use some help."

"Darla's helping Sam out on the property."

"*Your* help."

Why did she know he was going to say that? She'd never been clairvoyant before. She took a deep breath and asked, "What do you need?"

"Not much. Just a bag of powdered milk and a case of dry tuna noodles from the large pantry off the lodge kitchen. We're packing for our three-nighter."

"I'll have to bring Angie," Isabel warned.

"That's fine."

After she hung up, Isabel went out to explain the situation to Angie. Upon hearing that they were needed to carry supplies out to the campers, the little girl rushed inside, acting as if she'd been told they were headed for Disneyland.

"Can I bring it in my Barbie pack?" she asked, bouncing in place beside Isabel.

"Sure." Isabel helped the little girl strap on the pack, then chuckled at her enthusiastic skipping that lasted all the way to the supply room. Soon, she and Angie had packed the items and started down the tree-lined path to the cabins.

Trevor was standing near the picnic tables, dressed today in a navy shirt and long green pants. He was holding a clipboard, checking some list while talking to a couple of kids. When he saw Isabel and Angie, Trevor separated himself from the group. "Hey, ladies," he called out.

Isabel stopped on the path in front of him and stood *noticing* him. His deep green eyes. His luscious chest. His sensual mouth.

He stared at her lips.

She wetted them with her tongue, remembering.

Someone cleared his throat.

Isabel peered beyond Trevor's shoulder, into Dusty's pink face. "Hi, Dusty. How are you?" she said, and knew her burning cheeks must match the color of the young man's.

"Fine."

"Good."

Why wasn't he leaving?

He pointed at the carton of tuna noodles. "Can I take that from you?"

"Oh, here." She lifted it across.

"Thanks."

He left, but Isabel had already noticed that several

of the younger camp kids had stopped whatever they were doing to watch their leader.

Trevor turned toward the group. "Have you guys met Isabel and Angie?" he asked.

Isabel had recognized a few faces from mail and message deliveries, but she didn't know all the boys. Their answers confirmed this fact, so Trevor looped an arm around Isabel's waist and pulled her close. "This is my good friend, Isabel Blume. The half-pint over there is Angie."

After a chorus of hellos, Trevor directed a teasingly stern look at the few boys who still watched. "Do you want to go on this overnight trip or not?"

Several of them answered in the affirmative.

"Better get those packs loaded, then," he said, and handed the clipboard to Dusty. "Your counselors will come check them in a few minutes."

After the kids had returned to their tasks, Trevor tugged Isabel closer and said, "Hey, I've missed you. How've you been?"

She didn't have time to answer before Angie broke in. "Mr. Trebor, I carried your bag. See?" She turned around so he could peer inside her backpack. "'Cept I don't see how it can be milk cuz it feels like that stuff Isabel uses to make Snicker-noodles."

"Snicker*doodles*," Isabel corrected. "Are you think-ing of flour?"

"Yep. That white stuff."

After a final, warm squeeze that left Isabel glowing again, Trevor let go of her waist and pulled the bag from Angie's backpack. "This is a lot like flour," he said. "But if you mix this powder with water, you get milk."

"Can it make chocolate milk?" Angie asked.

"If you add chocolate, I suppose," he said as he hefted the bag onto a shoulder. "Dry milk doesn't taste as good as real milk, but it's a lot easier to carry."

"I know," Angie said, her hands on her hips. "I carried it all the way from the pantry."

"Did you, now?" Trevor said, pivoting to put the milk bag into a large frame pack behind him.

"Where you gonna take your dried-up milk?" Angie asked.

Trevor turned and knelt down in front of Angie, then pointed to the far end of the cabins. "See that path, between the two tallest trees?"

Isabel studied the thicket beyond the cabins and saw a place where the grass had been worn away.

"I see it!" Angie said. "Where's it go?"

"It leads to the same river that runs behind Sam and Darla's house," Trevor said. "We'll cross the water on a rope bridge, then we'll hike about three more miles to our campsite."

"Can I go?" Angie said, her expression hopeful.

"Oh, but this is an all-boy hike," Trevor said. "You probably know how bossy boys can be sometimes."

"R.J. thinks he's the boss of the whole U.S.A."

"R.J. is your brother, right?" Trevor asked.

"Yes. He gotta have S'mores every day at his sleep-away camp, but I bet he didn't get to carry dried-up milk."

Trevor nodded. "He missed out on a very important

task," he agreed. "Tell you what. The boys and I will return on Monday afternoon. What would you say about you, me and Isabel taking a hike that evening? We can search for hummingbirds and marmots, and you can carry our dinner in your backpack."

"I can?"

"Sure."

"The *whole* dinner?"

"All of it."

"Are we gonna go on the rope bridge?" she asked.

"No. I have another place in mind for our hike. A special place, where these boys won't get to go."

Angie clapped her hands over her cheeks and jumped around in circles. Then she stopped and frowned at Isabel. "I can't wait to tell R.J. Can I call him today?"

"Tonight after dinner," Isabel promised. She'd need to talk to Darla today about the change in plans concerning Angie and then let Roger know.

Trevor stood up and eyed Isabel, then Dusty called out to him. "Hey, Trev. We checked every pack, and they are all fine. We'd better hustle if we want to make it to the site by dusk."

Isabel noticed then that the dozens of teenage boys were milling around, apparently waiting for their director to quit chatting up the female visitors.

Oops.

She caught Trevor's eye and waved, then took Angie's hand to return to Darla's office.

Isabel shared Angie's disappointment about being left behind while the guys walked over a rope bridge and into adventure. But she had Monday evening to dream about.

After Angie had finished talking to her dad and R.J. that evening, she accepted Sam's offer to teach her how to play checkers. Darla had gone to Greeley to take her mother to dinner, and wouldn't arrive home until late tonight.

Faced with an unexpected block of free time, Isabel relaxed in her room and telephoned Josie. Her baby sister had a hundred male friends and was a master flirt.

She might have some good advice.

"You busy?" Isabel asked as soon as her sister answered.

"Not really," Josie said. "I just took a call from a woman wanting a baby quilt—I told her about the delay, and now I'm waiting for Gabe. We're headed out to grab a sandwich."

"Have you taken a lot of Blumecrafts calls?" Isabel asked.

"Some. Most people must know you're on hiatus, since you left the info on your Web site and answering machines, but the baby-quilt lady was disappointed. Her daughter's due to deliver on August first."

"Could you get me her number?" Isabel asked, thinking she'd call the woman. If she bought a second sewing machine, she could work from here as easily as she could work from home.

"It's downstairs at your computer," Josie said. "I'll e-mail it. Was that all you needed?"

Josie sounded rushed. Isabel would call back another

time to ask her sister to ship some supplies. For now, she'd get to the point of her phone call. "A quick question before you go?"

"Shoot."

"How's this flirting thing supposed to work?" Isabel asked. "I must be handling it wrong."

Josie chuckled. "How can a person flirt wrong?"

"They can flirt with someone who lives a long way from home. They can flirt when they are committed elsewhere."

"It sounds as if you do have the wrong idea," Josie said. "Flirting implies fun. As in short-term and anything but serious."

"Doesn't it turn serious?"

"Izzy, you hooked up with Roger right after Mom died. You need to see what else is out there before he gets lucky and slips a ring on your finger."

"Should I worry about the kind of person I'm flirting with? I mean, how much am I supposed to like them?"

"Person? You're supposed to flirt with people."

"I'm flirting with a person."

"Who?"

Isabel hadn't talked to either of her sisters about Trevor since things had heated up between them. She was unsure about her feelings for him, except that she admired him more each time she saw him, and felt more mixed about what she was doing.

And wanted to kiss him more.

Her thoughts felt private. Deliciously private. But she needed advice.

"Trevor Kincaid," she said.

"The rude guy?"

"He's not rude anymore. He's strong and patient and...confusing."

"Listen, Gabe just rang the doorbell and I've got to run. Is Trevor your type?"

"Do I have a type?"

"Born mother?" Josie said. "Go for husband material?"

"He's not that."

"Then you're fine. My best advice to you is to have fun, but to stay uninvolved emotionally. You can do that. I'm around guys all the time and I manage."

Isabel thanked Josie and hung up.

She stared at the phone and knew she was already too involved in some ways.

She should have called Callie. Her serious-minded sister had been involved with only one man in her entire life. She'd married the guy and, with a slight interruption, had stayed married to him for ten years so far.

She even had a little boy, so her experience with males was more in depth than Josie's. She might offer sage advice. Isabel dialed again.

"Callie, it's me. You busy?"

"I'm watching Luke make a total mess of his bowl of potato salad," she said.

Isabel pictured her sturdy, two-year-old nephew with his fists and face covered with the gooey dinner.

God, she'd just realized how much she missed him. Callie and her husband, Ethan, as well. And Josie. And R.J. and Roger.

She missed home.

"What's up?" Callie asked. "Are you homesick, sweetie?"

"Yes, but that's not why I'm calling." She hesitated, then said, "Things are just different here. Hard in a way, and sometimes I'm not sure what I'm doing."

"Is the professor still acting rude?"

"On the contrary."

"Oh, no."

Isabel still wasn't ready to confide the full extent of her trouble to her older sister. She didn't want Callie to warn her that she shouldn't be kissing some guy she'd met on her vacation.

She'd only done it once, anyway.

But she wanted to kiss him again, very much.

"Izzy, you are too sheltered," Callie said, obviously guessing about Isabel's silence. "I'm sure Mom never thought hard enough about what she was doing, keeping us isolated the way she did. As a consequence, Josie fills her time with party guys and I fell in love with the first boy who talked to me."

"You don't regret falling in love with Ethan?"

"Are you kidding? He keeps me sane. That's beside the point," Callie said. "The point is, you settled for Roger too quickly."

"Roger's a nice guy."

"Yes, I know. But you aren't out there pining away for him, are you?"

No, she wasn't. Isabel had never turned around the equation, had she? She'd wanted Roger to miss her. She'd never thought of her missing him.

"I miss him," she said, perhaps a bit defensively.

"Do I hear a but?"

"Maybe."

Callie sighed. "I've decided that Josie was right, Izzy. You need to see what else is out there before you settle down."

This advice from her cautious older sister?

"But go slow," Callie added. "Take care of yourself. And think."

Callie thought she should test the flirt waters, too? Surely that was a clear sign that she should go ahead and kiss Trevor whenever the opportunity arose.

Isabel spoke to Callie for a few more minutes, mostly about Luke's potato salad antics. She spent the next few days working hard. She answered the phones, called the hundred-song DJ and contacted Josie about sending those Blumecrafts supplies.

She smiled a lot, and felt clearer-headed, as she anticipated the return of the camp kids and her hiking date with their able director.

AFTER HEARING A NOISE, Trevor glanced up to spy Angie peeking into his office again. He pretended not to notice. He would finish his work sooner if he didn't talk to her. This was the fifth time the kid had checked on him since he'd sat down at his computer a half hour ago.

"Is it time to go?" Angie burst out, as if she simply couldn't restrain the twenty-first asking of the question.

"Give me one more minute," he said. After typing his name and credentials, he pressed the send button, shooting his weekly newsletter out to the e-mail in-boxes of twenty-five campers' parents.

They'd made it to their site by dusk that first night, despite the boys' skepticism that they'd make it at all. They'd sat around on felled trees and boulders, talking about their goals for the camp. One brave kid had wanted to see a bear. Another boy had only wished to escape the house he shared with six sisters.

During that first day, all of the boys had learned to traverse an incline and appreciate simple food cooked over a packer's stove. By the end of the third day, they'd managed tougher mountaineering tasks and more important goal setting. Trevor felt as if their two-week experience might have an impact on their lives. That was the gist of what he had reported to parents in his e-mail.

And since he'd showered earlier and the counselors could handle the boys this evening, he was free for the night.

Trevor shut off his computer screen and eyed Angie. "I'm ready."

"Hip, hip, hooray!" she hollered, and hastened out to Darla's work area. By the time Trevor had turned out his light and followed her, she was already prancing around Isabel, who was waiting patiently in Darla's chair.

"Are you ready, Izza-bell?" Angie asked. "Mr. Trebor's ready an' I'm really, really, really ready!"

No kidding.

Isabel dropped her scissors and some yellow cloth into a basket and stood up, slipping an arm around Angie's shoulders. "Let's go."

"Hurray! We're goin' on a hike!"

Both of them smiled at Angie's enthusiasm. "We need to pack up our dinner," Trevor said. "Then I should drop by and tell the counselors I'm leaving."

"Boy, are you pokey!"

"Angela Kay Corbett!" Isabel scolded.

Trevor winked at Angie. "If you ladies wouldn't mind pulling together our dinner, I can talk to the guys at the same time and we can meet out in the hallway."

"Sure. We can do that," Isabel said. "What do you want?"

He stared at her, wondering if she had any clue about the wicked thoughts she'd summoned.

"For dinner," she added, glancing at his mouth.

She knew.

And Trevor preferred his answer to the other phrasing of the question. But he had invited Isabel and her six-year-old friend on this hike. He'd have to behave. "See what you can find in the fridge, and we'll also want something to drink."

They entered the long hall together, then Trevor crossed to the community room entrance and waved Isabel and Angie down the hallway. "We'll meet here. Okay?"

When he poked his head inside the huge room to search for a counselor, he was glad he'd sent the women away. The campers had gone wild. Some had showered and were using their wet towels for a towel-snapping fight. Others, still in their hiking clothes, were running around sniffing one another, trying to decide who smelled the worst. A couple of the kids were actually asleep. Not an easy task, he would think, with the noise.

"Hey, Dusty," Trevor hollered when he saw him. "I'm heading out."

The counselor came over. "Going out with Isabel?"

"I promised her and the little girl a hike."

Dusty nodded. "She's a great lady. You're lucky."

"I know," Trevor said.

And he did. He'd never have planned to deepen his relationship with Isabel during a two-week camp, but the forced physical separation had allowed him to clarify his thoughts.

He'd have to be careful with her. She was different—kindhearted, gracious. Open. Perhaps her childhood had protected her from the things in life that could harden a person. The *people* who could.

He wouldn't be the man to hurt her that way.

Yet he couldn't imagine breaking away from her. He'd started something—an awakening in her. Whatever Roger had been to her, he couldn't have known her deepest beauty. Trevor would be a fool to stop seeing Isabel now. He didn't know who would learn more from whom.

So he'd do what he always did with women and warn her: he wasn't destined to be a groom or a fiancé. He'd seen a lot of couples act as if they were happily married. Upon close inspection, however, he could find the cracks that would eventually wreck the relationship.

The best he could manage, with any lady, was this—committed for as long as the relationship worked, and then a fond memory. If she couldn't settle for that much, he'd have to say goodbye.

Heartache averted.

Right now he needed to get going before Isabel's freckle-faced buddy found him and asked him again why he was so darn slow. "We'll be out on the property for a couple of hours," he told Dusty. "Tell the other counselors to call the cell number if anything comes up."

"Sure thing."

When he turned to discover the hallway empty, Trevor decided to take advantage of the extra time. Returning to his office, he opened a desk drawer and pulled three candy bars from a private stash. After dropping them into a pocket, he returned to the hallway, where Isabel and Angie now waited.

"Did you find us some dinner?"

"Yep!" the little girl said. "I put it in my backpack. I'm gonna carry it all by myself."

He studied the small pink pack strapped to her shoulders. "Are you sure you put enough food in there? I'm a big guy and I'm as hungry as a bear."

"We got six samwiches an' a whole bag of carrot sticks an' three waters," Angie said.

He frowned. "Bet you forgot dessert, didn't you?"

Angie's face fell. "We didn't find anything in the fridge for dessert."

"Hmm. Well, maybe I should drive to the Lyons grocery store to buy a chocolate cake before we go."

The little girl stared at him, her brown eyes wide.

"If I drive fast, I could be there and back in an hour."

Angie pursed her lips and frowned, apparently weighing the benefits of dessert against the problem of a longer wait.

Trevor pulled the candy bars from his pocket. "Unless you think these will work."

Angie's mouth fell open, then she closed it and narrowed her eyes. "You were teasin' me!"

He grinned. "Yes, I was."

"Izza-bell always tells R.J. he'll get in hot water if he teases me," Angie said. "You wanna get in hot water wif Izza-bell?"

Trevor met Isabel's gaze, lifting his brows. "Oh, of course not," he said, even while sending the unspoken message, *Bring it on.*

Judging from Isabel's thoughtful expression, she'd received his communiqué. If he could have lured her to privacy now, she'd be warm to his kisses.

He'd better get that confirmed-bachelor speech out of the way as soon as possible.

"Think you can carry our dessert in your backpack, too?" he asked Angie.

"Yep."

"Turn around."

She did, and Trevor slid the candy in beside the cold sandwiches. Then he led his new hiking buddies outside, and started down the same path that led to the cabins. On the way, Trevor pointed out a place where he'd recently spotted some prairie dogs.

His comment led to Isabel's question about wildlife in the area, and Trevor explained that deer, black bears and raccoons often made nightly trips to the riverbanks near Sam and Darla's house.

"I see raccoons around my place," Isabel said. "But I'd have to go to a zoo to see a bear or a prairie dog."

"Sometimes I see pigs and chickens in my yard," Angie piped up.

Trevor stopped and turned around on the trail to peer at her. "Pigs?"

"Yep."

"*Pig* pigs, that go oink and roll in the mud?"

She giggled.

Isabel laughed, too. "Angie's dad's a farmer," she said. "He raises hogs and also keeps a few chickens."

"That explains it," Trevor said, snapping his fingers. "I was beginning to think that Angie was *teasing* me, and that next she was going to tell me she'd seen elephants in her yard, too."

Angie kept tittering as Trevor turned around and continued their hike. When they drew adjacent to the cabins, he veered off down a narrower path that would eventually lead to Sam and Darla's house.

A few years ago, Sam and Trevor had cleared the pines in a small, secluded area between the cabins and the house. They'd encouraged a few aspen trees to grow around the perimeter, then they'd built a gazebo and planted the area with a shade-hardy bluegrass. After tilling a few flower beds, they were left with an oasis of manicured lawn in the middle of the mostly wooded property.

"Wow, this looks like a castle," Angie said after she'd spotted the gazebo. She raced inside the structure and made a couple of circles around it, checking out the bench and the hanging pots full of flowers. "Can we have our picnic in here, Mr. Trebor?"

He'd hoped she would like it here. A six-year-old

wouldn't tolerate a true hike on rough terrain. "You bet," he said.

Immediately Angie found a choice spot on the bench and shrugged out of her pack. Pulling out one of the sandwiches, she promptly unwrapped it and began eating.

Isabel stepped inside the octagonal structure. "This is so nice!" she said. "Like a secret garden."

"You haven't been here?" Trevor asked.

"No. Darla kept saying she'd bring me and Angie out here, but she's been so busy." Isabel peered at him and shrugged. "She didn't want me to navigate the path alone, the first time."

Isabel set out the rest of their lunch, then sat down and grabbed a carrot stick. "I'm glad to know our friends will be saying their vows in such a gorgeous place."

"They're getting married out here?" Trevor asked.

Isabel frowned at him as he sat down beside her. "You don't know?"

Trevor grabbed a sandwich. "No, but I'd have figured it out in plenty of time. Remember, all I have to do is stand where the minister tells me and produce the ring at the appropriate time."

"Trevor Kincaid!"

He'd just taken a bite, but he asked anyway. "What?"

"You act as if your good friend's wedding will be nothing but a pain."

It would, he thought as he chewed, but maybe he ought to drop the subject.

"Actually, in a roundabout way, it was a wedding that brought me here," Isabel said. "They are so…hopeful, don't you think?" She gazed toward the aspens and crunched into her carrot stick.

Or…maybe it was time for that warning. He caught Isabel's eye. "My contracts students who go on to became divorce attorneys have every reason to feel encouraged, I suppose."

Isabel frowned at him. "You aren't suggesting that Sam and Darla are heading for divorce?"

"They may be the rare couple who makes it, but they are mature enough to know what they're getting into. You do know that half of U.S. marriages end in divorce, don't you?"

"Half survive."

"That's right. You are an incurable optimist," Trevor said. "Don't tell me. Your parents never divorced."

"As a matter of fact, they didn't." Isabel glared at him, then grabbed a sandwich.

Was she truly unaware of how tough marriage could be? Trevor's mother and father had started off each of their marriages believing that this was the one that would last. When he was a kid, he'd thought so, too.

For a while.

Sometimes a very short while.

"Do me a favor?" Isabel asked.

"Depends," he said, and winked at her. He didn't want to come off as a complete cynic, even if he was.

"Don't mention the *D* word again here, where our friends will be saying their vows."

There went most of his argument, and his opportunity to warn Isabel about who he was and what he could offer her. He shrugged.

"My mama likes weddings, too," Angie said. "She wishes she could do a bigger one 'cuz she wants new dishes. I chipped her sugar jar on Easter."

Isabel peered at the child. "Weddings are nice for better reasons than the presents," she said. "But if you remind me, I can help your daddy remember that your mother would like replacement pieces for her birthday and Christmas."

"Daddy doesn't buy Mama presents," Angie said, adding gravely, "They are divorced."

Despite a missed opportunity to push his agenda forward, Trevor chuckled at the mention of that word.

Isabel scowled at him.

"I know," she told Angie. "I meant that you and your brother could give them to her."

"'Kay." Angie brightened. "Can I have my dessert now?"

After Isabel's yes, Angie ripped the wrapper off her candy bar and dove in.

Trevor studied Isabel.

She was speaking to Angie now while they both looked around at the gazebo and grounds. Isabel was talking about portable chairs and flower bouquets and dresses. As she spoke about the upcoming wedding, she was animated. Maybe a bit wistful.

Trevor leaned back on the bench, crammed the end of his sandwich into his mouth and chewed.

Sleeping Beauty loved the fairy tale, he could tell, and she deserved to have what she wanted. Maybe

Isabel would be one of the few who made it work, with some lucky guy who wanted to try.

And Trevor?

Well, he'd have to find the strength to back away.

Chapter Eight

After setting Angie's book on the bedside table, Isabel turned off the lamp and tiptoed from the bedroom. Although she usually stayed close in case the little girl needed a drink or a comforting pat, Isabel had accepted Darla's invitation to join her and Sam tonight down at the riverbank. They had both assured her that if Angie woke up, they could see the bedroom light clearly from the window.

Isabel let herself out the French doors and headed for the grouping of chairs near the water.

"She's already asleep?" Darla called out as she approached.

"She is." Isabel spoke up to be heard over the sound of the rushing water. "All that fresh air today must have worn her out."

"I'm sure," Darla said. "Would you like a glass of chardonnay?"

Isabel accepted the glass of wine they must have brought out for her, then lowered herself into the chair next to Sam. It'd been a long day. Trevor had invited the entire household to go fishing with the second group of campers, about a mile upriver. They'd all been up and on the trail early, and they'd returned in time to cook their catch for dinner.

Darla and Sam looked beat, too. Darla had leaned back and closed her eyes, only bringing her hand up every once in a while to sip her drink. Sam stared out toward the river, also limiting his movements to the occasional tipping of his glass. They sat, not speaking, for a long while.

Whenever Isabel and her sisters got together, they wore sweatpants, ordered takeout food and talked nonstop. Their conversations covered the gamut from their jobs to debates about politics and philosophy.

This silent sitting felt strange, until Isabel realized how relaxing it was to enjoy the peace.

It was too dark to see much, but the soft glow from some garden lights allowed her make out shapes and faces, as well as hints of the glistening water between the trees. The babble of the river energized Isabel. The smell of the pines and even the slightly fishy water made her want to breathe it in and memorize all of these new sensations.

She reclined in her chair and watched the sway of the tree branches.

"Nice, isn't it?" Sam asked after a while.

"Heavenly. You're lucky to live here. Did Darla tell me you'd inherited this property?"

Sam gave her one of his slow, barely there smiles. "The acreage belonged to my mother's mother. Dad developed it into a ranch, then I added the lodge after he retired."

"Where are your parents now?"

"Tucson. Winters are hard on my mother's arthritis."

"And how did Trevor come into the picture?" Isabel asked. "You two aren't related, yet he runs the camp from here. Surely that setup is unusual."

"Trevor might not own the land, but he loves this place as much as I do."

"You must really trust him."

"With the exception of Darla, here, I wouldn't trust anyone else more."

Isabel wasn't surprised. Despite their bad start, she'd learned that Trevor was a fine person—probably better than he knew. "How did you meet him?" she asked.

But a sound had caught Sam's attention. He sat forward, peering into the distance toward the lodge.

Isabel stilled, wondering if the sound had come from an animal. Darla had sat up and opened her eyes, also.

But soon both of them relaxed in their chairs again, and Sam's next comment gave away the identity of their intruder. "Ah, come on. You don't want to hear any more about that old cuss, do you?"

Trevor appeared through the trees. "Should I worry that you're talking about me?"

"Damn straight you should worry," Sam said. "I could tell this young lady a few things, you know."

Embarrassed that she'd been caught asking about him, Isabel watched and listened while the two men traded barbs.

Trevor's hair was wet, and he had on light slacks and a dark, button-down shirt. When he claimed the chair next to hers, he gave her one of those sexy winks.

"I'll refill drinks," Darla said, standing to collect glasses. "Trevor, you want a glass of wine?"

"Man, do I! Thanks."

"I'll help you in the kitchen," Sam said, hastening to join his fiancée on her walk to the house and leaving Isabel alone in the quiet with Trevor. Finally alone, for the first time since he'd kissed her. Could that have been three weeks ago? She was beginning to think she'd dreamed the experience.

She wanted to kiss him again.

She couldn't just plant one on him. She wasn't the type, and heaven knew what he would think if she was that brazen. Heaven knew what he would do. Besides, Darla and Sam would be returning with the wine.

So she couldn't grab the guy.

"You know, you can just ask me if there's anything you want to know," Trevor said. "We don't need Sam or Darla to run messages between us."

"I wasn't prying for secrets," she said. "You were just on my mind, I guess."

"Then you'll understand what brought me over here."

How could he make her so nervous and so happy to be around him at the same time? She glanced at him. "I was asking how you and Sam met."

"Actually, we met through marriage," Trevor said. "My dad married Sam's older sister when I was about eleven. Sometimes she brought me out here to visit her folks, and that's when I met Sam. He would have been about twenty."

"Sam's sister is your stepmother?"

"She was for two years and nine months. Dad's on his third wife, now. Mary was number two."

"Wow."

"Anyway, Sam was working as a hand for his dad then, so he was here all the time. Despite the age difference, he and I hit it off. He took me fishing, taught me to climb. The friendship developed over the years."

"Is that another reason you started the camp?" Isabel asked. "As a payback for the attention you got from Sam?"

"Maybe that was part of the reason," Trevor said, peering at her.

Those forehead dents lined up in full force. Something about their conversation had disturbed him. Isabel wanted to ask, but Sam and Darla returned with two glasses of wine.

Just two.

And they had matching towels draped over their shoulders. "Are you guys interested in a late night swim?" Darla asked. "The water's heated."

Isabel accepted one of the glasses. "I need to be here in case Angie wakes up. You go ahead, though."

She glanced at Trevor then, communicating a silent message. *Stay.*

"I got enough water today when the kids pushed me in the river," Trevor said.

But Isabel sensed an echoed response.

He wanted to stay.

As Sam and Darla started toward the lodge, Isabel fended off another onslaught of jumbled feelings. She shouldn't be spending so much time with this guy while she was on her vacation. She shouldn't want to kiss him.

She smiled to herself. She might have the inclination to kiss first and talk later, but she couldn't hurdle the chair arms and get on with it.

She really was a small-town girl at heart.

"What other reason did you have for starting the camp?" she asked, because she was still curious about Trevor's choices. Parts of him didn't match up with others.

"Why does there have to be another reason?"

"I can't see that camp director fits your image."

"What image?"

"Boulder's most confirmed bachelor."

He gave her a funny look.

"You don't trust women."

"I trust women."

"Okay. You don't trust relationships. Maybe because your parents divorced so many times."

He gave a slight nod. "There you go."

"It's admirable that you devote so much of your time to those boys," she said. "It simply doesn't fit my picture of you. Men who don't want to marry don't want kids. And men who don't want kids don't spend a lot of time with them. And yet here you are."

Trevor looked disturbed. He set his wineglass on the grass at his feet and stood to face the water. "I don't talk about this often," he said. "But I suppose it's no big secret. Remember when I told you about Clair?"

"The girl you almost married at sixteen?"

"Yes." He hesitated. Shrugged. "She had the baby. It was a boy. Matthew."

Isabel set her glass down, too, and got up. After approaching Trevor from behind, she touched his shoulder.

"Wait a minute. You said nature took care of things. I thought —"

"I know what you thought," Trevor said, his voice rough. "The whole truth is tough to talk about. The baby died before he was a month old, just over fifteen years ago. Matthew would have been the same age as these camp kids. I don't need a therapist to tell me why I do it."

"What happened to Matthew?"

"He was born nine weeks early—exactly a week before Clair and I were to marry. His lungs weren't fully developed. A virus developed into a respiratory infection before he ever left the hospital. He didn't survive it."

Isabel stood behind Trevor, wishing she could wrap her arms around him. Feeling as if that, too, would be too bold.

And wondering why she fought her every impulse.

"I'm sorry," she said.

Trevor turned toward her. "Before Matthew was born, I'd wished so many times that Clair wasn't pregnant," he murmured. "That I could turn back time. And then, poof, Matthew was gone. Clair and I called off the wedding. I returned to my life." Though he looked at Isabel, his eyes held a faraway expression. Then his jaw clenched. "I got my wish."

"You were young," she said. "And you didn't wish for your son's death. You wished you hadn't made the mistake in the first place."

"Right." Trevor chuckled, but it was a humorless sound. "And now you know all my secrets."

"Not *all* of them."

"The most important ones."

She nodded, sympathizing with Trevor's painful past but also enjoying the warmth of his body heat so close to her.

So here and now.

"I can't believe how much I've told you about me," Trevor said. "Have I really only known you a month?"

"It was a major event in your life. Maybe you needed to talk about it."

"And maybe you're a good listener."

Isabel realized Trevor had focused on her. He was present in the moment, too.

And still very alone with her.

Isabel's world skewed slightly out of place, then, as her perception of Trevor changed. She was no longer only physically attracted to a guy who was sexy and exciting but not her type.

She was attracted to Trevor as a person. He lived the kind of big life she dreamed about. Some people might have drowned their sorrow in drink or drugs. Some might have hardened themselves to other children. Some might not have loved that tiny baby so strongly.

Trevor had, and he'd made the best of things. He had a huge heart for kids, even if he didn't know it. After he'd gotten over his initial moodiness, he'd been wonderful to Angie.

Being with him, even for one night, might break Isabel's heart. She should retreat to the house and work on the baby quilt—or any piece of busy work that would take her through such a dangerous night to the clearer thoughts of morning.

She shouldn't stand here, wishing even more than ever that Trevor would kiss her.

But when he moved forward, she did, too.

Her heart raced. She still felt the breeze against her skin, still smelled the trees and the water, but she saw only Trevor's face. His lips had parted slightly. His eyes gleamed brilliantly in the darkness.

She'd never forget this moment.

He put his hands on her upper arms, pulling her forward. Then finally he pressed his mouth to hers. His kisses began as pecks, but soon his tongue teased hers, plunging and retreating. His lips sucked gently, making her open herself further to him. Making her wish.

For more skin. More touches. More Trevor.

His arousal pressed against her belly, hard and hot. Her desire turned serious as she felt her lower muscles contract.

She forgot where she was for a moment. Forgot that she was in Colorado. Outside. Standing near a river. Flirting. Exploring. Learning.

She was aware of only *him.*

When his hands moved down to cup her bottom, pulling her tighter against his heat, she wanted to kneel down with him, right here, and discover if they were good at actions even bolder than kissing.

She couldn't do that. She and Trevor had met a month ago, and this was their second time kissing. Besides, she knew for a fact that flirting did not include sex.

Even Josie would say so.

So Isabel kissed Trevor one more time, then she backed away. She kept her eyes closed for a minute, making sure her legs were strong beneath her before she looked upon the face that would likely haunt her dreams.

Trevor opened his eyes more slowly, and even in the dim light she could see the desire in his expression. Could read it in his stance. She thought he might ask why she'd stopped, or try to kiss her again.

"You okay?" Trevor asked.

Oh, yes. She was okay. More than okay. She was floating. "Yes."

"I'll walk you to the door."

She frowned. Leave it to Trevor to surprise her.

They both grabbed their wineglasses and carried them to the house. After they reached the French doors, Trevor stopped and stood away from her, his arms and face rigid. "I'll say good-night here."

She must have looked confused, because he answered the question she hadn't asked. "I love kissing you, but I'm thinking we ought to quit while we're ahead."

What? Why?

"Right," she whispered.

"You live in Kansas. We want different things."

Now she asked it. "We do?"

He smiled. "The other day at the gazebo, I realized that you are exactly the kind of woman who should get married. You'll make some guy a beautiful bride."

She couldn't imagine marrying anyone if it meant saying goodbye to Trevor now.

"Maybe," she said.

Was that what this night was about? Why he'd walked over here? Was he saying goodbye?"

"I live here," he said, peering into her eyes. "I'm happy, here. And I'm not sure we can keep this casual."

"I know." She wanted to smooth her hand along his brow and tell him not to worry so much.

"But I'll be thinking about you, over in Kansas. You're not the kind of woman a man forgets."

"I'm not leaving, Trevor."

"Yet."

And that was it. Isabel studied his face for a moment, seeing a ton of regret in the set of his jaw, and knew he was right.

She said good-night and walked inside.

She'd head home to Kansas soon. Home to Roger and choices that had once seemed perfect for her.

It was a good thing Trevor was busy with the summer camp, because separation was exactly what she needed. Not because things had cooled off and she wanted him to recognize what he was missing. That was Roger.

With Trevor she needed the separation because the feelings between them raged too hot.

"WHEN MY GREAT-AUNT stays over, she sleeps in Daddy's bed an' he sleeps on the sofa," Angie said as she and Isabel sat across from each other at Sam and Darla's kitchen table. "Is that what you're gonna do?"

Isabel watched Angie pick the streusel crust off her cranberry muffin and pop it in her mouth. "What do you mean, hon? Why would I stay at your house overnight?"

"'Cuz you'll be married to my daddy. He said so."

Isabel nearly choked on her coffee. "I'm sorry," she said, working to control her sputtering. "But please explain."

"When I talked to Daddy last night, he said he really, really misses bofe of us. He might even marry you."

Isabel frowned. She hadn't spoken to Roger last night, choosing instead to dial for Angie and wander down the hall to watch television with Sam and Darla. She wasn't quite sure what to say to Roger. She certainly didn't want to tell him about her summer here. She didn't want to ask about his, either. So she avoided him.

Roger existed in Isabel's real world. Trevor was a part of a dream summer she'd never forget. Isabel didn't need her mother or sisters to explain the difference.

"Daddy asked if we were ready to come home, but I said we were having too much fun fishing and hiking and ever-thing." Angie had finished the top of her muffin and was eyeing Isabel's.

Isabel pushed her plate across the table to Angie.

Her plan was working. The guy who she'd wanted to propose to her for over a year might very well be planning to propose to her. She should be happy.

But she could only think about Trevor.

It was a good thing he'd begun another two-week camp session today. From the sound of things, he'd be very busy with this oldest group, and she wouldn't see him much.

"Hurry and finish, hon," Isabel said. "I promised Darla I'd sit in the office this morning. She and Sam are going to town to look at tuxedos."

"What's a tusk-ee-doe?" Angie asked.

"That's tux-ee-do. It's a suit that a man wears to a wedding or a formal occasion."

"Will Daddy wear one to your wedding?"

Why did Angie keep bringing up weddings on a day when Isabel didn't want to think about them? For her whole life, Isabel had dreamed about her big day, and suddenly the thought of rings and proposals made her feel nauseated.

"If your father gets married again, he might wear one," Isabel told Angie. "But I don't know if he will get married again, to me or anyone else."

Angie frowned.

"It's okay, hon," Isabel said. "Just remember that no matter what happens, your parents and I will all love you."

"Mama and Daddy said that when they got a divorce."

"That's because it's true, Ange. Now, let's get your things and go see Darla."

"'Kay." Angie's brow was still pinched as much as a six-year-old's could pinch, but she managed to cram the rest of Isabel's muffin into her mouth.

"And we don't need to talk about weddings again today, okay?" Isabel said. "I'm tired of talking about them all the time."

"Ffll-kay."

Isabel helped Angie gather a few books and toys, then they wandered down the path to the lodge.

Darla was on the phone when they walked in, but she hung up at once. "My cousin's coming to the wedding. So far, I've counted sixteen yeses and four nos."

"That's great." Isabel hoped Angie would remember their nix-on-the-wedding-talk agreement. She didn't want to know if Roger had made a recent conversion from never-again to possibly-very-soon.

Not now.

Angie had plopped down in her bean bag chair and was unzipping her backpack.

"Are you feeling all right, Miss Angie?" Darla asked. "You don't usually make such a quiet entrance."

"I'm not sposed to talk about weddings, so I'm quiet 'cuz you're talking about weddings."

Darla directed a puzzled look toward Isabel.

Isabel rolled her eyes and shook her head.

"All right, then." Darla peered at the little girl. "Well, Miss Angie. If you are interested, I was wondering if you'd like to take a drive with me and Sam in a while."

Frowning as she removed a doll from the bag and then rummaged inside for its missing shoe, Angie asked, "To see the tusk-ee-does?"

Again, Darla frowned at Isabel.

"Tuxedos."

"Oh!" Darla nodded. "Yes. We do need to go into the bridal boutique so Sam can check the fit of his suit." She approached Angie and bent down to whisper, "My wedding's coming up in three weeks, did you know that?"

"Yep."

"And since you'll be here, I had an idea. Would you like to be my flower girl?"

Eyes wide, Angie gasped. "A real flower girl, wif flowers to throw on the floor?"

Darla chuckled. "I take it that's a yes?"

Angie nodded, beaming.

"Good. Then we can pick out a dress today," Darla said. "And next door to the boutique there's a bakery that has the best cherry pie in the whole U.S.A."

Angie jumped around the office.

"Darla, you don't need to take her," Isabel murmured a few minutes later. "I know she'll need a dress, but I could take her to town later this week. You and Sam will get the chore done quicker without worrying about her."

"Why would I want the chore to be quick?" Darla asked.

"Because you have enough to worry about with your mother's illness and the camp."

"The camp's going well and my mom is fine today," Darla said. "I spoke to her this morning and she had plans to go to a movie with some friends. She feels better on the days she doesn't do chemo."

"I'm glad," Isabel said, but something Trevor had said to her once kept running through her mind. She didn't want to take advantage of Darla's graciousness. "But you're still very busy. I'll keep Angie here."

"Isabel, stop. Sam and I will enjoy Angie's company, and it's only right that we pay for the dress."

"I'll buy it."

"It's my wedding, and I'd have had to reschedule if

not for you," Darla said. "So shush! Besides, Trevor called."

That statement halted Isabel's arguments.

Darla stared at her. "What's wrong?"

"Just finish what you were saying."

"He wondered if you could join him and the campers today."

Why?

Isabel clamped her jaw and frowned at Darla.

She'd never told her friend that she and Trevor were anything more than acquaintances, so she couldn't ask the hundred questions running through her head.

"What's wrong now?" Darla asked.

"Aren't the campers going off-site today?" she asked.

"They're taking the bus over to a canyon where there are some good, fairly easy climbs for the campers to try."

"Climbs?"

Darla explained. "Rock climbing. You know, you strap into a pulley system and climb the rock face, then rappel down."

Isabel knew about climbing. She simply couldn't believe Trevor would ask her to go with the group. They'd said an early goodbye, and he couldn't actually need her help.

"There's nothing to climb in south-central Kansas but ladders and stairs," Isabel said. "I couldn't be much help. He must be mistaken."

"I know you've never climbed, my dear. That's why Trevor and Sam and I agreed you might like to try it."

Isabel stared at her friend. "It can't be safe for a total novice to help the kids with something so risky."

"Oh, no! Trevor is an expert, and all of the counselors are seasoned climbers. You're to go experience it, not teach it."

Okay. So, for whatever reason, Trevor was reversing his earlier intention to stay away from her. He was asking her to go.

She wasn't sure she'd be smart to go. She was halfway in love with him, and thinking she'd probably go home to Kansas and forget about men completely.

All of them.

Forever.

She'd be a spinster.

"Isabel!" Darla's brows had lowered over her hazel eyes, and she shook her head. "You have an opportunity to experience an adventure today. Why aren't you excited?"

She'd also have an opportunity to feed her obsession for Trevor. She'd caught a glimpse of him late last Thursday afternoon as he'd played soccer with the boys and she'd taken another hike to the gazebo with Angie.

She knew he'd seen her. He'd watched for a moment before some lanky kid had kicked the ball toward the goal and he'd had to dive for it. But he hadn't acknowledged her.

She'd seen him again across the lodge dining hall on Friday night, and they'd both simply nodded.

The man was driving her mad with his switches from hot to cold and stop to start.

She was driving herself mad.

If she didn't find out what he wanted, she'd go crazier, wondering.

She should go. Ask questions. Find out.

At Darla's suggestion she changed into lightweight pants and hiking boots, then said goodbye to Sam, Darla and Angie before she left for the cabins.

When she approached the clearing in the path that allowed her to view the gathering of males down at the picnic tables, she picked out the tallest, darkest head and homed in on Trevor's grin.

For four days she'd craved that smile. Now it only vexed her. Was he trying to make life difficult?

The climb would be a challenge. She'd be silly to think it'd be easy. The bigger problem, however, would be understanding Trevor.

But she would.

Before she agreed to this climbing trip, she would know what was in that man's head.

Chapter Nine

"I'm glad you decided to come," Trevor said as he met Isabel on the trail, away from the others.

"I have to admit I was surprised by the invitation." She peered past his shoulder at the camp kids. The group was growing louder and larger as the boys finished dressing and met near the picnic tables.

"Don't be," he said. "I just thought you might enjoy a day away from the office and Angie."

Isabel held his gaze. "I'm still not sure I'm coming," she said. "Why don't you tell me what you're doing first?"

He'd forgotten how she cut right to the chase. Hard for a guy to maintain a protective wall when a woman cut right to the chase. "I'm inviting you to come climbing with me and the campers," he said.

The easier part of the truth.

"What's different about today? Yesterday we didn't say boo to each other."

He shrugged. "Yesterday I didn't have a group climb planned. It'd be a shame for you to return to Kansas without trying your hand at it." He tried a smile. "It's my favorite sport."

Isabel kept frowning at him, obviously refusing take the invitation at face value. "Why do I get the feeling you're always holding something back?"

She was tough.

"Honestly? Inviting you was a spur-of-the-moment decision," he said. "Darla told me that the few lodge guests had checked out this weekend, and that she and Sam were planning to take you and Angie to Boulder. You've already been shopping several times."

"So you told Darla I should climb with you and the campers. I get that. I still don't know why you went from goodbye forever to…to *this*. And I don't know what this is, other than a climbing trip."

And he still wasn't going to tell her.

He wasn't sure.

Only—

He took in her eyes—sleepy blue, even though she was angry. He scanned her unbelievably soft lips.

They parted.

Was that another invitation?

Should he kiss her again and distract her from her tough questions? Distract himself from his confusion?

But Isabel peeked over his shoulder again and stepped backward, as if she was suddenly aware that they weren't alone. "We should be careful. I didn't tell Darla about the other night."

He hoped not. Sam meddled enough already, and Trevor was still too confused to handle Darla, who'd probably tell him to be good to her friend, or else.

"So when Darla said you wanted me to come with you today, I couldn't tell her that it wasn't a good idea, and I couldn't ask her if she knew why you keep changing. So I really don't know what you're doing." She paused for a breath and then asked, "What are you doing, Trevor?"

Okay. So her attention hadn't been diverted. But he still couldn't tell her what he was doing.

He hadn't forgotten her. Hadn't done anything but handle what he needed to for the camp, and wonder where she was and what she was thinking.

But if Isabel complained today about the tough climbs, her scraped ankle or the camp-style lunch they would eat later—anything—he might be able to manage his thoughts about her. He might convince himself to let her go home with regrets that weren't overwhelming.

"I realized our goodbye was premature," he said, offering the truth because she wouldn't let him get away with anything else. "You're still around and I can't pretend you're not. But realize we'll have thirty chaperones today." He shook his head. "No repeats of the other night."

"Of course not," she said, but she glanced at his mouth again, then looked in his eyes, brows lifted.

Waiting for what? Hadn't he just explained?

"We really need to head out or we'll lose the cool of morning. Do want to come with us or not?"

She glared at him. "You're not going to tell me why you invited me, are you?"

"I did."

"You are a very aggravating man, do you know that?"

He turned on his heel, returning to the clearing and cursing himself for giving in to another stupid impulse. The woman's tenacity was frustrating.

Well, hell. She could follow him onto the bus or not. He'd deal with her choice, either way.

He approached the kids, motioning with a wave of his hand that it was time to hike out to the parking lot and load up. He led the group without allowing himself to peek back and see if she was following. When he reached the bus, he climbed on board and into the driver's seat.

As the kids piled on, they made an awful racket. This was the group's first day together, and apparently they were getting along well. Camaraderie could be earsplitting.

Trevor watched the door of the bus, cursing himself for doing so. He counted the kids and counselors as they climbed the steps. He knew when every kid was on and had found a seat. He knew when it was time to close the dadgum door.

But he watched it. Waited. Gave her that last half a minute to change her mind.

She did.

He saw her appear from behind the side of the lodge and jog toward the bus. She gave him the slightest nod as she came aboard. Then she greeted some of the guys before she sat down about four seats back, next to a beaming Dusty.

Hallelujah!

And damn it. He'd just realized.

He'd never have driven away and left Isabel here. He'd have hopped off the bus, kissed her senseless and hauled her onto it. He hadn't wanted her to come along with him today so he could find some fault that would enable him to keep an emotional distance.

She'd probably back down once she saw the rock face. A lot of women would, and that didn't matter.

He wanted her to come because he enjoyed being around her. He liked her looks, he liked her attitude, and he even liked the way she called him on his bull.

He'd been disappointed in himself, for giving up so easily. For refusing to accept the challenge of loving a woman who might very well break him of his cynicism.

Damn it, some part of him still wanted to believe in the fairy tale.

As Isabel watched the scenery through the bus window, the angry buzz in her head was overtaken by excitement about what she was doing today.

She'd never dreamed she'd have a chance to try climbing. Josie, the most athletic of the Blume sisters, had learned to ride a jet ski and fish and even hunt, but she'd never climbed. And Callie had once lived in Colorado, but she'd only learned to snow ski.

Isabel couldn't wait to tell her sisters about this. She'd been amazed, during her stay here, that keeping in touch via telephone calls had been so easy.

She couldn't wait to try climbing.

"Have you climbed before, Dusty?" she asked her seat mate.

"Sure. I grew up in Boulder," he said. "My Scout troop took a couple of climbing excursions every year. I can't wait to see Trevor in action, though. The Walters brothers told me he's amazing. Can scramble right up the toughest face without a rope."

Isabel glanced toward the front of the bus and realized Trevor was watching her in the rearview mirror.

She averted her gaze. "You use ropes, then," she said to Dusty. "I wasn't sure. Except for what I've seen in magazine articles, I know very little about climbing. Tell me how it works."

Dusty explained that Trevor was taking them to an area known as Button Rock, and that the camp kids had already spent an hour this morning learning how to attach the ropes and clips that would keep them safe from falls.

She frowned, wishing she'd been in on the training. Would she learn enough at the last minute?

One of the kids who'd been sitting up front got up and walked down the narrow bus aisle, stopping to crouch down next to Isabel. "Trevor asked me to switch places with you."

She looked at Trevor again, but he was concentrating on the road as he steered around a curve.

Isabel had considered ignoring him today, to pay him back for refusing to answer her question.

But when Trevor met her eyes in that mirror and simply nodded, she knew she should go up there and hear him out. "See you later, Dusty."

She got up, allowing the skinny blond kid to slide into her seat, then walked to the front to sit in the vacant space behind Trevor.

"I overheard bits of your conversation with Dusty, and I didn't want you to worry. If I'd thought of inviting you earlier, I'd have involved you in the training."

"Then you are planning to let me climb?"

"Sure. If you still want to try it after you see what it's like. No pressure."

Isabel fell silent. She was comfortable with the thought that Trevor would keep her and everyone else safe from harm. She did trust him in that way. He was sharp, and he seemed to consider every potential problem before he committed himself or anyone else to a plan.

Maybe that was why he kept changing on her.

Perhaps he kept thinking about pitfalls.

"In the three years we've been running the camp, we've never had a climbing accident," Trevor said, apparently mistaking her silence for worry. "A few sprained ankles, a snake bite, some mild dehydration— boys are awful about neglecting to drink water—but we've always had safe climbs."

"Trevor, I'm not worried. I trust you to get us all through this day without so much as a scratch."

He said nothing.

She thought he didn't believe her. "I can't wait to try climbing," she added.

"Really?"

"Really."

"Good." He caught her eye in the mirror and gave her a little wink.

That simple facial movement was enough to get her going again, about why he'd asked her to come today.

As a friend who knew she'd soon be leaving, as he'd suggested, or as a man who still wanted more from her?

She still wanted more from *him*, damn it.

Those thoughts carried her along the highway until finally Trevor made a left turn into a lot, parked the bus and opened the doors so the boys spilling into the aisle had an outlet.

Isabel hiked to the site between two seventeen-year-old campers who maintained a steady dispute about which one of them was going to climb the toughest face the fastest.

Within a half hour, three eager boys were strapped into the harnesses and climbing the rock face while most of the group waited at the bottom. Trevor had scrambled up first to attach the rope systems, amazing everyone with his ability to do so without the aid of ropes.

Isabel had known he was fit, but she was as impressed as everyone else.

Two counselors had climbed up after Trevor, and they waited for the boys from above, while Dusty and the Walters brothers stayed below to keep a firm grip on the ropes, also making sure the harnesses were secure before the boys started their climbs.

Climbing was followed by rappelling down, and the boys' hoots indicated that they were having a blast.

Isabel was content to wait her turn. After all, the enthusiastic teenagers were the ones who had paid for an outdoor adventure. About a half hour before lunchtime, however, Isabel realized that their day was going to be cut short.

Thunderheads were forming out to the west of the canyon and moving in fast. "Has everyone had at least one turn to climb and rappel?" Trevor called out after two of the older campers had made their way down.

The consensus was that they had.

"Good, because we're going to have to quit now." As the kids groaned their disappointment, Trevor caught Isabel's eye and winked again.

Wow. Two winks in one morning. Was this one a conciliatory wink? A promise of some kind? She really needed to figure out the man's winking system.

"We can come out here again on Friday morning, if you aren't too tired from our overnight trip," Trevor told the group. "For now, let's head back to the cabins and get packed. Your lunch is on the bus. Go eat, and I'll be there in a while."

Isabel was disappointed, but she understood Trevor's dilemma. Maybe she could return with the campers on Friday. One of the counselors began to lead the group to the bus, and Isabel fell into line.

Trevor caught her shirtsleeve and tugged her backward. "Hey, didn't you want to try this?" he asked.

"Now?" She eyed the backs of the others, who were well on their way up the path. "Is that possible, with only the two of us here?"

"I can handle the belay alone, if you want to try it." He peered at the clouds. "I'd say we have about a half hour, which is enough time for you to get up and back down."

She scanned the tall rock face. "Won't the group be waiting for us? For you?"

"The kids will be on that bus eating lunch and bragging about how great they did. Think of a strong peanut butter smell, mix it with the odor of sweat and toss in the collective boasts of thirty seventeen-year-old boys."

She grimaced. "Well, when you put it that way, I suppose I don't have much choice."

"Do this if you want to, Isabel. I'm only teasing," Trevor said. "I'll just grab the equipment, if you prefer."

"I'd be disappointed jf I didn't try this."

He nodded, his gaze steady and...something else. Affectionate? Respectful?

Something.

She wished she could read his thoughts. He helped her strap into the system, and she was glad the boys weren't around to watch when he put his hands near her thighs to fasten her into the harness.

Isabel was intensely aware of her sexuality.

He finished, giving the rope a soft tug to test it. Then he turned to her, the look in those dazzling green eyes saying the very same thing she was thinking—let's forget about the climb and continue the touching instead.

But he stepped away. "Go ahead when you're ready," he said. "There's a good handhold up on the right, and you can go from there. After you get up top, wait for me. You can rappel down, then I'll unfasten the equipment and follow you."

Isabel frowned at the rock, finding the small notch in the boulder that he'd mentioned. She moved up about five feet, then had to study the rock before she found places off to the left to continue.

She loved the challenge of finding the perfect holds for her hands and feet. Of moving upward, past places where she had to stretch for a tenuous hold to move forward.

Although she knew Trevor was down below, keeping her safe, she was thrilled when she crawled over the top without once needing him to use the pulley system to catch her.

The view from the top of the cliff was gorgeous. Behind her, another boulder continued upward. Before her, the face dropped about thirty feet and was surrounded by forest.

She wanted to shout from her high and lonely perch that she'd just climbed a freakin' Colorado boulder.

She would have, too, if she didn't think the busload of boys could hear her.

Within minutes Trevor had scrambled up behind her, and he grinned immediately when he saw her face. "Guess I don't have to ask what you thought about that."

"Oh, man! It was wonderful! Almost like finishing a complicated piece of stitching or conquering a difficult math problem."

He frowned, cocking his head. "I've never heard climbing compared to sewing, but I know what you mean. It's satisfying. A victory."

"Right!"

"Right." He studied her, his expression sober. When he moved forward, she recognized the look in his eye.

She intended to kiss him back.

His lips were warm, salty, loving. There was nothing

tenuous about this kiss. He meant to communicate his desire for her, and she returned the same message to him. She opened her mouth to him, accustomed now to the natural sensuality of his kisses.

She bit into the firm flesh of his lower lip, then felt her tummy flip when he growled. When his tongue tipped against hers, she met it eagerly. She was hungry for anything this sexy, enigmatic man had to offer.

Unafraid, in this moment, to take him on.

His hand moved along the side of her ribs, then gently cupped her breasts. Instead of batting his hands away, she moved her own hands around to his muscled back, leaving herself open to him.

She wished they were touching bare skin.

He moved his thumbs across her nipples, teasing them while desire shot through her limbs like lightning.

After a moment, he stopped kissing and looked down at her breasts. His intent expression weakened her knees.

"Why do I want you so much?" he whispered. "Why can't I tell myself we're wrong together and go on?"

A fat raindrop splashed against Isabel's cheek, cool and refreshing. Another hit her arm. Then her wrist. Then the top of her head.

As if he would be willing to wage a battle with all-powerful nature for this particular moment, Trevor scowled toward the sky.

A drop clouted him on the nose.

Isabel chuckled.

"I don't think we'll get these sprinkles for long," he said, returning his gaze to her. "We'd better hurry down."

Even though she was disappointed, Isabel grinned. "What's so funny?"

"Think the heavens are trying to tell us something now?"

He lifted a brow. "Do you believe in that kind of cosmic message?"

"Not really," she said. "But if I did, this'd be a biggie."

The rain started to fall more heavily now, streaking down in silver daggers that would soak them if they didn't move quickly. Trevor turned to adjust the ropes and pulleys.

"Are you comfortable with rappelling down?" he asked as he stood up, beside her. "Remember that you control your speed by releasing the rope behind you."

"I watched all morning. I can do it."

With deft fingers, Trevor checked the harness and gave her a nod. Isabel immediately backed off the wall and moved down the face by bouncing her feet against the rocks.

Climbing was better, but she loved rappelling, too.

Moments later Trevor followed her with the ropes and clips fastened around his waist.

He was about three feet from the bottom when the clouds opened up. "Let's go!" he hollered. He jumped down, grabbed her hand and ran along the path, slipping here and there on the muddy ground.

Isabel found something about the situation amusing. Maybe she simply felt exhilarated. She'd done something amazing today, with an exciting man.

She'd felt brave in every way.

Her smiles turned to chuckles as they continued along the path. By the time they were close enough to see the bus, they were both drenched and she was practically in stitches.

Although Isabel could see only silhouettes through the bus windows, she knew the boys must be watching.

She pulled at Trevor's hand, communicating that he needed to slow down.

He did, peering back at her even while he continued walking. "You okay?"

"Just need a moment to get control," she said. "Thanks for staying behind so I could try climbing. I had a great time."

And then they were at the bus door. Trevor paused to let her board first, and his expression made it clear that he'd had a great time with her, too.

Chapter Ten

After pulling a long T-shirt over her swimsuit, Isabel slipped into a pair of sneakers and sat at the edge of the bed, anticipating Trevor's arrival. They'd both left Sam and Darla's backyard about fifteen minutes ago, after joining the couple and Angie for a S'mores cookout.

She and Trevor had made a date for a late-night swim lesson. The thought freed butterflies in Isabel's stomach, but she wouldn't miss tonight for anything.

While Sam had helped Angie toast her marshmallows, she'd invited him to watch *Shrek* with her—he'd never seen it. Isabel and Trevor must have both recognized the opportunity. They'd traded glances, and soon he was suggesting that they forgo the movie viewing for another lesson.

Despite their turmoil, she and Trevor needed something from each other. What exactly, Isabel didn't know, but she hoped they could learn to trust their most basic feelings for each other.

She wanted the experience of knowing him better.

A knock sounded at the door.

Butterflies thrashing, Isabel crossed the room and opened it. Trevor looked tall, hot.

Intentional.

She got goose bumps.

After grabbing a towel and comb, she followed him out through the garage and across the darkened path to the lodge. She might have been tempted to fill the silence with chatter, but she was too nervous. This was the first time she and Trevor had made arrangements to see each other for the specific purpose of being alone.

Poolside, Trevor flipped a switch on the lodge wall. Isabel dropped her towel onto a chaise longue and stood looking at the water, sparkling like an aqua gemstone under the light. "Think it's cold?" she asked, dipping her toes in.

"The pool's heated," Trevor reminded her. "But we can sit for a minute, if you like."

They sat down, side by side at the edge, their feet swishing through water that felt warm against the evening breeze. Isabel wished she didn't feel so tongue-tied.

How did she start this? *What* was she starting?

"This isn't easy, is it?" she asked.

"Jumping in the pool?"

"Learning to trust someone."

He frowned. "You having trouble trusting me?"

"I trust you in a lot of ways," she said, studying their legs: his tanned, muscular, slightly hairy; hers pale and small in comparison. "I knew you'd catch me this morning, if I fell."

He didn't try to fill the silence.

"The complications are hard to ignore," she said.

"I know."

"We're agreed, then. We need this." She wouldn't define *this*. He knew. "But we know whatever happens is only for now."

"Are you all right with that?" he asked.

"I have to be."

He glanced at her, then stared at the water. "That's how I feel. You don't really fit with my plans—not the ones I set a long time ago—but I don't want to let you go."

Exactly.

And now Isabel felt a larger quaking in her belly. One problem had been solved, presenting another.

"There are a lot of things I've never had the opportunity to do," she said. "I haven't dated much."

"Why not?"

"No opportunity, really," she said. "My mother always swore men were evil."

Trevor glanced at her, frowning. "But what about your dad? Didn't you say once that they'd never divorced?"

"They didn't." Isabel dug her toe into the water and flipped a spray of droplets into the distance. "I suppose they didn't need to because neither of them ever wanted to marry again."

Trevor put his arm behind her, leaning back. Leaning nearer. "Is your dad around?"

"I assume so. I don't know."

"No contact?"

"None. He left when I was very small." She launched another foot-blast of water. "So I didn't have guys around. By the time I was old enough to care very much, Mom got cancer. I kept busy taking care of her. Then she died."

"Did you date then?"

"Roger."

"Wow." Now Trevor kicked a spray out, too, sprinkling the opposite side of the pool.

"So, I've had one first date, with a neighbor I already knew." Isabel leaned back to look at Trevor. "How does it work? What do people talk about on first dates?"

"If they don't already know each other, they start with basics. Their jobs, their histories, their hobbies." He shot her a leer. "Unless they *really* hit it off."

She rolled her eyes, then used her foot to splash water toward his face.

"Hey!"

"Hey, you."

He put his hands up, as if surrendering. "I was only going to say that then they'd talk deeper. Hopes. Philosophies. Fears."

Isabel studied their legs again. "What are you afraid of, Trevor? Besides marriage."

"My problem with marriage is mostly intellectual," he said. "Maybe the human animal isn't designed to stay with the same lover, forever."

"Then answer my question."

He bumped his arm and shoulder against her side. "My fear?"

"Yeah."

"Being wrong. Missing out."

An unguarded answer to a tough question.

This was her favorite version of Trevor.

"What's *your* biggest fear?" he asked.

Easy.

"Not finding someone. Being alone."

The silence grew old. Heavy.

Trevor pitched headfirst into the pool, sending cold water fountaining onto Isabel's torso. She sucked in her stomach and gasped as she watched him swim away a few yards, then flip around beneath the water.

When he popped his head out, he grinned at her. "Your best dates will know when to break the tension." He waggled those brows. "Take off that wet shirt, come in the water and tell me more about yourself, bay-bee."

His silliness eased any hesitation Isabel might have felt. She tugged her shirt off, then slid into the water and his embrace.

"Think we can continue our conversation like this?" he asked, his voice low as he draped her legs over an arm.

"Why not?"

He moved her into deeper water, then dropped her legs but kept his arms around her. "All right. Tell me something surprising about Isabel Blume."

"I've been downhill skiing."

He lifted his brows. "I had the impression you hadn't been anywhere."

"Callie lived in Denver with her husband for a while. The Christmas after my mother died, Josie and I went to visit and we all took off for a day to go ski at Winter Park."

"Did you like skiing?"

"I loved it after lunch. In the morning I spent too much time disentangling my legs from my skis."

He laughed. "Everyone does."

"Now *you* go. Something about you."

"I've been downhill skiing."

She cupped a hand to shoot water at him again.

He laughed again, eyeing her, then sobered as he moved a piece of hair away from her mouth. "I'll tell you a hope."

"Shoot."

He tugged her close, and she could feel his arousal. "I want you."

"Mmm. I want you, too," she murmured.

His lips caught hers, rough and warm. He moved his hands to her hips, cupping her bottom as he pulled her upward.

She wrapped her legs around his waist, then felt his mouth leave hers to kiss the skin above one breast.

Warm heat filled her lower belly as her body prepared for his loving. Their sexes were separated by the flimsy material of their swimsuits.

It would be so easy for her to slip out of her clothes.

So easy to answer some questions for herself.

Once again, Isabel couldn't believe her own boldness. She wanted to touch Trevor. Wanted to discard their suits and straddle him. Wanted to accept his hard length inside herself and take on the challenge of a deeper experience with a man she'd never forget.

Damn it, she was going for it.

As TREVOR FELT Isabel's hands move downward, their target obvious, he was both shocked and pleased. Yet he caught her hands and brought them to his mouth.

He teased her fingertips with his lips and tongue. Delaying.

He burned too hot to let her touch him, and he knew they should move. They were too near the lodge and cabins, where dozens of teenage boys were playing cards, eating junk, hanging out after a hot, tiring day.

Any of those kids might suddenly appear poolside.

He lifted Isabel into his arms and started for the ladder. He thought he could hang on to control long enough to lead her down the hall to his room.

Where he could close and lock the door.

But Isabel pressed both palms against his face, turned his head and kissed him, her mouth wet and open. She'd learned to use her tongue and mouth to tease.

He forgot to move for a while. And now that his hands were occupied with holding Isabel, she slipped a hand inside his swim trunks. Determined, obviously.

Damn. He couldn't risk them being caught.

Dropping her legs so she could stand again, he caught her hand. "Not here. Some of the kids are in the lodge."

She glanced toward the building. "Good heavens." She stepped away from him.

Her eyes were wide, her lips swollen. Small wonder he'd been so tempted to forget responsible behavior.

"I don't mean to insult you by this suggestion," he said. "But we could go to my room."

Isabel had crossed her arms in front of her breasts, and he felt a sharp regret that she was moving away from that relentless desire. "But your room is in the lodge," she whispered. "The kids won't barge in?"

"Hell, no. The door has a lock."

Trevor eyed the pinkness of Isabel's cheeks. She'd never in a million years go into that room, knowing that the kids might come along and knock or holler for Trevor to come play air hockey.

When they might make assumptions.

He was glad she was like that.

He was also as frustrated as hell.

He shrugged. "I can't invite you back to my Boulder house, tonight—I need to stay on Burch property—but I wish we could be alone."

"I do, too."

"I want to be free to love you," he said, and although the timing was bad, he asked the question screaming through his head. "Are you going home to Kansas right after Sam and Darla's wedding?"

"I'd planned to," she said. "They'll be leaving on their honeymoon, and I need to get Angie home to her dad."

So she wouldn't be free to visit Trevor at home. He wondered if he should even entertain the thought that she might take the little girl home, then fly back to spend time with him.

Or that they could start some long-distance phone relationship that couldn't possibly satisfy but would at least be contact.

Trevor slicked a hand through his hair, regretful as his body cooled and his arousal loosened.

He needed it to loosen.

He needed to do the right thing.

He wasn't sure what that was.

"So it's that room down the hall from the camp kids. Or we kiss but don't touch?" she asked.

"Or we stop completely."

She moved forward, leaning near his ear. "Guess what?" she whispered. "I'll take the kisses."

"Thank heaven."

She looked at him lovingly, and he was tempted again.

"Just a minute," he said. He swam to the side near the lodge, then pulled himself out of the water and turned off the lights. "This okay?" he asked. "It may not be private, but it's better than having the dadgum spotlight on us."

"Good idea."

He crossed to the pool in five long strides, dived in and came up at her feet.

"I really meant to learn how to do that."

"And I meant to teach you. We just got over here and—"

She put a hand over his mouth. "Please. I'm doing what I want to do."

"Come here, then."

She wrapped her arms around his shoulders and stretched up to him, meeting his lips with hers. Trevor communicated his feelings with only his mouth for a good, long while as they moved slowly, weightlessly along in the water.

When water lapped against his upper abdomen, Trevor felt free to brush his fingers against Isabel's submerged breasts. No one could see. No one would know except the two of them. He slid his fingers beneath her suit. Her nipples were firm and slick. Perfect.

He wanted to see her.

He moved her swimsuit aside, then ducked his chin beneath the water long enough to kiss her there. To nuzzle her gently before coming back up to watch her body respond.

He kissed her harder, plunging his tongue in her mouth while he moved his thumbs against her bare nipples.

"Hey, Izza-bell and Mr. Trebor. We're goin' on a moonlight swim, too!"

As soon as he heard that voice, Trevor moved to block the view of Isabel, waiting for her to adjust her bathing suit.

He glanced across.

Angie was standing at the edge of the pool, wearing her little orange arm floats. Her face looked…excited? Curious? He couldn't tell, but he thought she must not have seen. It wasn't quite light enough for her to have seen much.

"You okay?" he murmured to Isabel.

She nodded, and he turned around but continued to stand between her and the little girl. "Hi, Angie. Decided to join us, did you?" he asked.

"Yep. Dah-la's coming, too. She went to get some extra towels out of the laundry room." Angie leaned forward a bit. "I can't see, 'cuz it's dark. Did you learn to swim yet, Izza-bell?"

"Not yet." Isabel moved to stand beside Trevor. "I'm still working on floating."

"Mr. Trebor needs to teach you kicking. 'Cuz it didn't look like you were kicking."

"Maybe that's what I need to do."

Darla appeared outside the lodge doors, her arms full of folded white towels. "Hey, you two," she said. "We don't mean to barge in, but the movie ended and Angie didn't act at all tired. We hope you don't mind if we join you for a lesson." She moved to the lodge wall and flicked on the light.

Trevor didn't answer her. He couldn't have given her an honest answer. He did mind, very much.

But she didn't know about him and Isabel. Heaven only knew how Darla and Sam had managed to stay in the dark.

Angie started chattering about the movie, and the evening passed and so did Trevor's desire. Again.

For now.

He stayed for about an hour, managing to work with Isabel on her kick without embarrassing himself, and then he made his way into the lodge while she returned to the house with Darla and Angie.

As he lay in his bed, he tried not to picture Isabel there beside him. He could imagine having her next to him every day. When he went to bed. When he woke up.

He could imagine wanting her there, even past the time when this fierce need for her waned. When sometimes just talking was enough and sometimes it wasn't.

Maybe he'd been wrong.

Maybe loving was worth the risk.

* * *

SHE FELT SOMETHING warm and breathy, against her cheek.

A deep, soft murmur. "Isabel."

She smiled. Dreaming of Trevor.

A hand on her shoulder. Shaking her. "Isabel!"

She opened her eyes to the darkness and a shape she couldn't see as much as sense. "Trevor?"

"Shh! Come on." He took her hand, tugged her away from her cot.

Isabel sat up and peered over her shoulder at the bed where Angie lay with her arms and legs tangled in the covers. Fast asleep. She got up and followed Trevor out the open bedroom door into the hallway.

He closed the door behind them.

"What are you doing?" she whispered.

He gazed at her, his eyes tired. "Carving out some time with you."

She frowned down the silent hallway, lit by a couple of sconces. It was very quiet. "Is it morning?"

"Four o'clock."

"Four o'clock! Trevor!"

He tugged her into a hug. "Shh! Remember I'm directing a summer camp. The kids and I are leaving at seven, heading for a three-day campout." He stepped back to peer at her. "I'll be busy with this oldest group. We tackle bigger challenges."

As she awakened, her brain kicked into gear. "And after these campers leave, Darla and Sam will get married."

And I'll go home.

"So, a date at four in the morning?" she mused,

peering toward the closed bedroom door. "Think Angie will be all right?"

Trevor frowned. "Does she usually wake up at this hour?"

"No. And if she did, Darla would hear her calls."

"Then she's fine." Trevor bent down to pick up a folded blanket and vacuum flask, then handed her a paper sack. "Carry breakfast?"

She took it, and followed him toward the private exit.

Before she stepped outside, however, she glanced down at her cotton gown. "Hey!"

He turned in the doorway. "What?"

She swept a hand down her gown. "I'm not dressed."

"You're decent." He moved his glance down and up. "Besides, it's warm outside and no one will see you."

She followed him, trying not to giggle.

When they were outside and headed toward the forested part of the property, she asked, "Where are we going?"

He turned around and gave her a half smile. "To my favorite place here at Sam's."

He led her toward the gazebo, finding his way even in the dark shadow of the trees. He knew Sam's property well. Again, Isabel felt safe in his company.

After they reached the aspen clearing, he veered down closer to the river and looked upward. "This is the spot."

Isabel looked up, too. She could see the quarter moon through an opening in the trees.

Trevor spread the blanket, then took her bag and the

flask and set them on the ground. The flask fell over. He moved it, but it fell again. "The ground's sloped," he said. Finally he walked a few yards nearer the tree-lined river and set them on a rock.

Isabel dropped down onto the blanket and lay on her back. She folded her hands behind her head and closed her eyes.

"Hey, you can't go to sleep on our date!" Trevor said. "Want me to pour you some coffee?"

"Not yet." She kept her eyelids shut. "Too early, and the ground is more comfortable than my cot."

"Why are you sleeping on a cot?"

She felt him move down next to her, and opened an eye, peering at him. "I could get poked all night by six-year-old elbows, listen to a squeaky cot all night while Angie thrashed around, or sleep on the cot."

"I guess you could sleep now, if you want."

She nodded, closing her eyes again. Relaxed.

He groaned, low and long. "*I* can't sleep, though."

Isabel sat up halfway, glancing at the fly of his jeans. Was he turned on, uncomfortable, at this hour? Had he brought her out here to—

He laughed. "I didn't bring an alarm clock."

"Oh!" She flopped back down.

"If I miss my six-o'clock wake-up call, the entire camp might stage a manhunt for their missing director."

She could hear the smile in his voice. She lay looking up at that slice of moon. "It's nice out here, at this hour."

"I know."

"So how is this your favorite place?" she asked. "Did you used to bring girls here in your reckless youth?"

"No."

"Why, then?"

"Honestly? I just found it today."

"Trevor!"

"It'll be my favorite place from now on."

"Aww. That was nice." Isabel turned toward him, resting her jaw against her hand so she could study Trevor's profile. "You know tomorrow's Independence Day?"

"I do."

"Are you doing something special with the camp kids?"

He moved nearer to her, pulling her torso against his. She nestled her cheek against his chest, wrapped her arm around his belly.

"Yes, but it'll have to be a natural celebration," he said. "We can't shoot rockets up here. We'll probably roast hot dogs. We might go tubing in the river."

"Sounds great."

"And I know *you* have plans to head to Boulder, to eat dinner out and watch some parade."

"That's right. For Angie. We're also taking Darla's mom, if she feels like going."

"Did you celebrate holidays in your house?" he asked.

"They were very low-key." Isabel lifted her head to peer at him. "We made gifts for each other at Christmastime. I hated it then. I felt lonely, seeing the same three people all the time. Doing the same things." She lay back down. "Now I think it was kind of nice. My sisters and I carry on a few of the old traditions."

"Sounds good to me."

"What about you?" she asked. "Darla told me you have a bunch of stepsiblings. Did you have huge family parties?"

"That depended on whose house we were at, and how the parents were getting along. Sometimes I was around a crowd, sometimes I was the only kid. Holidays were never the same from year to year."

"I guess they wouldn't be." She looked at him as he stared at the morning sky, recognizing that their different experiences had made them feel the same—alone. Lonely.

"Could you imagine living here, Isabel?" Trevor glanced at her and away.

But she felt it.

He wanted her to stay. He wanted more time.

He couldn't come right out and ask, because he wasn't offering more than his time and company.

She sat up, bending her knees and curling her arms around them. "That'd be hard for me. My sisters and I have a special bond, because of the way things were. I love my life in Kansas."

He'd sat up, too, leaning back on his hands with his legs stretched out beside her. "I can tell."

Isabel frowned, feeling as if she wasn't saying exactly what she meant to say. "I wish I could stay," she said. "I feel something special for you. And…well, sometimes I feel as if I'm living a fragment of the life I could."

"But?"

"Why give up something I love?"

"The grass is greener theory?"

"Exactly." She rested against his legs, happy he understood. "And where I live, how I live—that's what makes me who I am."

He lay back down, settling his head on his hands, looking relaxed and okay with what she'd told him. "So we'll just have to enjoy the time we have left."

"I guess so."

"It's a date, then. Four o'clock, here, every day."

She laughed, then dived on top of him, matching hip to hip and chest to chest. "I'd do it."

"I would, too. But you know I'll be away. I have an obligation."

"I do know. It's okay."

She kissed him, this time with fun, smacking kisses. She liked their playfulness because it lifted her gloomy thoughts of goodbyes.

Their kisses grew sensual, and he explored the flesh beneath her gown as she eased her body to fit his awakening one.

She heard a small sound. A scurrying.

Trevor flipped her around next to him and looked toward the riverbank. Toward the trees and the rock.

"What is it?" Isabel said, staring.

"Shh! Look."

Twin lights lit the darkness. Eyes, staring at them. Remembering their discussion of bears, Isabel moved closer to Trevor. "What is it?"

"A bold raccoon, after our breakfast."

Isabel felt frightened, even though she'd chased off plenty of raccoons at home. But there, she was generally inside her doorway with a pan and spoon, trying to frighten the animals away from her trash can. Here, she was in that raccoon's territory.

"Come here." Trevor stood and held out a hand, then led her backward, toward the gazebo.

They sat on the long bench, yards away from their blanket, and watched the animal rummage in the bag. The big 'coon tore at the paper until it found a muffin. It nibbled a moment, narrow eyes watching them, then held the food in its mouth and trotted toward the trees.

Isabel let out a breath. "He was so big!"

"I think she's a she. Look." Trevor pointed again, slightly to the right of the place where the raccoon had gone.

She could see them, under the limbs. As the mama raccoon scurried along a path to her hideaway, a row of babies followed along behind her.

When they were out of sight, Isabel breathed again and turned to beam at Trevor. "What a fun date, Trevor!"

"Fun? She took our breakfast," Trevor said. "And I *knew* better than to leave food out."

"I'm not hungry."

"I'm not, either, but wait here." He walked across the grass, grabbed the flask and torn bag and carried it back. "Want coffee now?"

"Lord, yes."

He poured coffee into the lid and they took turns sipping as the day grew light. They didn't talk anymore or continue with their kissing. Again, just sitting together was enough.

Isabel thought if she were a different person—less a homebody and with a different set of experiences behind her—she might have said yes to Trevor today.

She might have moved out here to Colorado and stayed for as long as their romance lasted.

He was right, though. They didn't have long. They should take great care and enjoy each other in the time they had left.

Chapter Eleven

Isabel coaxed the roots of a dandelion from the ground beneath a clump of bachelor's buttons, then sat back on her heels and tossed it onto a growing pile of yard debris behind her.

"This area could use some mulch," she told Darla, who was working on a flower bed nearer the gazebo. "I doubt that any more weeds will sprout in the week before your wedding, but the beds would appear more groomed."

Wiping her brow, Darla said, "Good idea. The mulch bags are in the lodge storage room, though. I should have thought to bring one out."

"No problem. I'll find them." Isabel got up and stretched her muscles, then watched her friend work for a moment. "Anything else you need?"

"Since you asked, I could use a cold drink," Darla said. "This part of Colorado rarely sees ninety degrees, and I guess I'm not used to it."

Darla was a strong woman, but the stresses had begun to affect her. She'd been quieter than usual lately. "Are you okay, otherwise?" Isabel asked.

Darla glanced over her shoulder. "I'm fine."

"You and Sam okay? Your mom?" Isabel prompted.

Now Darla stopped working and turned toward Isabel, shielding her eyes from the sun's glare as she looked up. "Mom was very tired the last time we spoke. The day before she was great. Do you remember seeing that kind of up-and-down change when your mom was sick?"

Isabel knelt beside Darla. "Yes, I do. But remember she didn't accept medical treatment, so after a while it was all downhill. Toward the end she was very frail and small. Almost like a different person."

"I'll bet," Darla said. "I can't imagine how I'd feel if my mother had refused treatment."

"Your mother's doctors think she'll kick the cancer, don't they?" Isabel asked.

"Yes. And I think so, too." Darla returned to her work. "Now that the last camp session is over, I just need to get through my wedding day. When Sam and I get on that plane to Alaska, I'll relax."

"I know you will," Isabel agreed, standing up. "Now, I'll go get that mulch and a big glass of something ice-cold for you."

"I'll come help you carry." Darla dropped her trowel.

"Stay there, Darla," Isabel said. "I'll bring Angie back with me, and she can carry the drinks in her pack. Those counselors have enough to do without keeping track of a six-year-old."

"It's their last day. I'm sure they don't mind. Anyway, Sam's hanging out with the guys today, and I know he'll watch out for her."

Perhaps. And this summer, quite a few of the folks up here had developed an affection for Angie. She was in Isabel's care, however, and Isabel wanted to make sure that no one shouldered the responsibility for her longer than a few hours at a time.

"I told Angie earlier that we might be able to use help with watering out here," Isabel said. "She'd get a kick out of working that well pump."

Darla returned to her work. "Good point. Bring me some iced tea."

As Isabel made her way over to the lodge, she pulled her hair from a band at her nape and regathered it into a neater ponytail. It was definitely hot outside today. She was sweaty from her weeding, but she felt fine.

She'd inherited a love of gardening from her mother, and ninety was pretty average for July in south-central Kansas. The heat reminded her of home.

It was hard to believe she'd be returning in just over a week. She missed her sisters and friends, and she was ready to start in on some orders that had come in for Blumecrafts. She'd finished the baby quilt.

She would be pleased to be home.

She hoped.

She'd come to view Darla and Sam as the extended family she'd never had. And she hadn't even let herself think about leaving Trevor.

Checking her clothes, Isabel realized she was filthy. With dirt-blackened knees and a T-shirt that was no longer white, she could only imagine about the parts of her she couldn't see.

Trevor and the campers had returned from their

mountain-climbing excursion early this morning. She'd already run into Trevor twice, and he'd been bright-eyed, watching her.

She might see him at the lodge.

Oh, well. He didn't strike her as the kind of man who would notice a few dirt smudges. Besides, she wasn't supposed to care.

She entered the lodge through the nearest entrance, then checked the laundry room for Angie. A few tokens were spread out over the tray of the machine, but the room was vacant. Earlier, the little girl had been taking turns playing the video game with Sam and Dusty.

Isabel walked down the hall to search in the community room. The boys were loud in there, probably exhilarated about their climbing experience and also anticipating their parents' arrival in a couple of hours. She spotted Dusty, talking to a couple of the boys, and asked if he'd seen Angie or Sam.

"Angie had a phone call in the offices," Dusty said. "I took her over there a minute ago and told her to meet me here."

"And Sam?"

Dusty beamed. "At the house, wrapping and hiding Darla's wedding gift from him."

Grinning, Isabel continued on to the office.

She heard the little girl crying before she saw her. She rushed into the room and found Angie in Darla's chair with the phone receiver cradled to her ear.

"Daddy, I'm sposed to be the flower girl," she said. When she saw Isabel walk in, her brown eyes widened.

"No," she said then, her expression stubborn. "Yes.

She is. 'Kay." She took the receiver away from her ear, and without a word handed it across to Isabel.

Isabel pulled the phone to her face. "Roger, what on earth is happening? Your daughter is very upset."

Roger didn't hesitate or try to explain. "As soon as I hang up, I'm calling the airlines. My daughter needs to come home immediately."

"What happened?" Isabel's heart raced. "Is R.J. okay?"

"He's fine. Everyone is fine. But Angie needs to be here with me." Roger's voice was cool.

Strange that he'd decided such a thing this late in the summer. The little girl had barely a week left. It would be much easier, not to mention cheaper, for Isabel to bring her home in the car.

"Just a moment," Isabel said to Roger, then covered the mouthpiece with her palm.

She smiled at Angie, who was sitting at Darla's desk, trying to be calm but hitching her breath every few seconds. "Hey, hon. Do me a favor, would you? Find Dusty and ask him to wrap one of those brownies we made yesterday. Put it in your backpack."

Angie nodded, visibly calmer.

"Now, can you remember this?" Isabel asked. "Also get a bottle of *iced tea* for Darla and a juice for you. Carry it all out to the gazebo. Darla's there. You know the way?"

"Yep."

"Okay. Tell Darla you're there to help water the flowers, and that I'll come along in a couple of minutes."

Angie hopped out of the chair. "I like brownies."

"Then tell Dusty you need two."

"Okay!"

Isabel watched the little girl exit the room, satisfied to see the half skip the child started on her way down the hall. Then she leaned against the desk and returned the phone to her ear. "Okay, Roger. Tell me what happened. Why is Angie so upset, and why are you deciding now that she needs to come home?"

"Because I want my daughter here with me."

"But when Darla realized that Angie was going to be here for the wedding day, she asked her to be the flower girl. She bought her a dress and ordered special flowers. Angie's looking forward to it."

"She'll get over it," Roger said. "She shouldn't have been there with you, anyway. I had no idea, Isabel, that you could be so careless."

Isabel frowned. "Careless, how?"

"When Angie spoke to R.J. a couple of nights ago, she asked him if he thought it was okay for you to kiss other boys."

"Other boys?"

"Some counselor there. In a swimming pool."

Oh, no. Angie must have seen her and Trevor on their nighttime swim, after all. Isabel felt awful. If she'd known that the little girl was worried about it, she would have tried to explain.

It was too late for that. What surprised Isabel now was that she didn't feel particularly remorseful about Roger. Confused, certainly. Maybe a little angry. But not as sorry as she should be, considering.

"Why is this coming out now, Roger?" she asked. "Angie saw us days ago."

"R.J. didn't think that much about it," Roger explained. "He said he thought Angie had confused something she saw. Yesterday he mentioned it in passing because we stopped by the Git-n-Go and talked to Sandy for a while."

"Sandy?"

"The clerk. Curly red hair? Short and skinny?"

Isabel remembered her. The woman had always had her eye on Roger. Finally he'd noticed?

Isabel's guilt lifted some, but strangely she didn't feel jealous.

"So R.J. mentioned Angie's comment to you, and then what happened?"

"I stayed up all night, thinking about it, and then I called Angie just now. She said she saw you in the pool with some counselor. Said you were kissing like TV people, and she wasn't sure if it was okay but she didn't want to get you in hot water."

"That wasn't a counselor, Roger. It was Trevor, the camp director and Sam's good friend."

"So it is true."

"Yes, it is."

Roger sighed. "I'll book a flight for tomorrow, and call you when I know a time. If you'll get her to the boarding gate, I'll have an attendant waiting for her."

Now he finds a way to get Angie home.

But Isabel's bigger concern was for the little girl. "Roger, she's six years old. You can't put her on a plane alone."

"She won't be alone. You'll be at one gate and I'll be at the other. In between, a flight attendant will sit with her. When Barbara decided to move to Texas, she explained that we could send the kids back and forth this way."

"But R.J. will be with Angie then," Isabel said. "She's too young to handle a plane trip alone, even with a flight attendant watching over her."

"She's too young to watch her father's girlfriend kiss some other guy."

"We broke up."

"I thought the breakup was for show," Roger said. "The kids do talk to me, Iz. I knew you wanted to get married. R.J. said he thought you were expecting a proposal after my cousin's wedding in April."

"And *I've* been operating under the assumption that we would continue as we were—just boyfriend and girlfriend—or not at all."

"Under the circumstances, I'd say it's the not-at-all option. Wouldn't you?" he said.

Isabel could insist that the opposite was true—that she hadn't gone to unforgivable lengths with Trevor. That she'd left a thread of lifeline intact.

But she didn't bother. "*You're* breaking up with *me*, now?"

"Guess so."

Isabel felt a twinge of something. Not hurt. Guilt? Disappointment? Maybe it simply felt strange to abandon a hope she'd clung to for so long. "Anyway, I'm sorry Angie was confused," she said. "We hoped she hadn't seen us."

"We? You mean you discussed the possibility with...him?"

"Sure I did," Isabel said. "We didn't know how long she'd been standing there."

"So the...*it*...went on for a while."

Isabel tried to ignore the pain in his voice. She reminded herself that Roger hadn't wanted to commit to her. That he had begun to neglect her. She tried to figure out what her sisters would say.

And she knew this as truth: what she'd done or hadn't done with some other guy was not Roger's business. He'd never taken on the task of *making* it his business.

Isabel was tired of letting him control this conversation. Right now she wanted only to make Roger understand that Angie didn't deserve to be penalized.

She wanted to be a flower girl at the wedding of a couple who had been kind to her this summer. "I don't see what it can hurt to let Angie stay until after the ceremony," Isabel said. "I'll bring her home by car, and we can talk about things, or not."

"I want her home, Isabel. I wouldn't have let Angie go away on vacation with a woman I didn't care for. One I didn't trust."

Ouch.

"I'll call you with flight details," Roger said, sounding curt. Tired. And then the line clicked and buzzed.

He was gone.

Isabel reached behind her to drop the receiver in its cradle, then stood leaning against the desk as waves of emotion hit her.

Guilt about Angie's premature departure.

Regret about kisses she didn't want to regret.

Worry about Darla and her wedding plans.

And, yes, pain.

A movement caught her eye, and Isabel looked up as Trevor crossed the lodge porch and poked his head inside the door.

"Hey, what are you doing in here?" He stepped inside and closed the door behind him. After crossing the space in long strides, he bent down to kiss her, hard and hot.

"God, I've missed you," Trevor said as he backed away. Then he frowned at her expression. "What's wrong?"

"Angie's dad called," she said. "Angie saw us in the pool that night. She said something to her brother, who said something to Roger."

"That's too bad," Trevor said. "But surely it's okay. I know young kids are uncomfortable when they see kissing, but we weren't doing anything wrong."

Isabel held his gaze. "Roger wants me to send Angie home."

"He should want her home. She'll be there in a week."

"He wants her to come now. Tomorrow."

"Why?"

Isabel scowled. "He's mad at me for kissing you."

Trevor returned her scowl. "I thought you told me that you and Roger broke up."

Isabel didn't want to explain to Trevor that Roger had understood the breakup to be a persuasive tactic.

She didn't want to risk adding Trevor's pain or anger to her mix of woes. "We did," she said.

Trevor studied her face. "Was Angie upset?"

"She was worried. She'd like to see me and her father get together."

"Is that wishful thinking on her part, or does she have a reason to believe you will?" Trevor's green eyes glittered with questions.

Tired of weighing which things would hurt and which wouldn't, Isabel decided to relax into the whole truth. She hoped she could trust Trevor to handle it well.

"I wanted to marry Roger," Isabel said. "We'd dated for a long time, and I felt taken for granted. So yes, I had hopes that he'd miss me and ask. Angie knew that, I think, although I never said so specifically."

The dimples lined up. "And what did Angie's dad want?"

"He wanted nothing to do with marriage until after I came here."

Trevor lifted his brows. "And then?"

"And then he started talking differently."

Trevor nodded, looking away. "Early on, I had the idea you were omitting a few details about Roger. Guess I was right."

"Trevor!" She sought his gaze, but he avoided hers.

"We knew our time was limited, right?" he said. "Nothing was lost. Don't worry about it."

She didn't answer. Couldn't have spoken even if she'd known what to say.

A lot was lost, and Trevor should recognize that.

Whether they'd talked about a future or not, she'd made a connection with him. At the very least, she'd thought she had another good friend here in Colorado. She'd imagined phone conversations. E-mails.

She'd imagined irreplaceable memories of a man who thought of her as fondly as she thought of him. She'd even imagined another heart-to heart about a possible future.

Trevor glanced at her then, his expression distant. "Too bad about Angie," he said. "Let me know when she's leaving so I can say goodbye."

Isabel watched him stride out the door, then she stood away from the desk and realized her legs were shaking. She dropped into Darla's chair and shoved her palms across her eyes. She was still sitting there moments later, when Darla walked in.

"Angie said she has to go home?" Darla asked, her hazel eyes round with concern. "What happened, Izzy?"

"She saw me and Trevor …" Isabel paused. Had she learned nothing about discretion? "Where is Angie?" she asked. "I don't want her to hear."

"Sam's taking her to Lyons to get the makings for S'mores and hot dogs. She wants a cookout on her last night." Darla sat down at the desk Isabel had been using this summer. "Now, tell me. Angie saw you and Trevor doing what?"

"Kissing. In the pool. Maybe doing a little more than kissing. I don't know how much she saw. But she told her dad and he isn't too happy with me."

Darla snorted. "Serves him right, if you ask me. If

he wanted you for keeps, he should have made sure you knew it."

"I know."

"Then what is it, Izzy?"

Isabel sighed. "If Angie leaves, you'll have to change your wedding plans."

"Angie was a last-minute addition," Darla said. "We asked her to participate because everyone else here is in the wedding party. But the only necessities to my wedding are that Sam and I say our vows and trade rings. We'll be fine."

"I'm glad to hear you say that," Isabel said. "But I also hurt Angie. She wanted to be in the wedding."

"I already told her she could take the dress and flower basket home," Darla said. "If you plan a back-to-school party and invite some first-grade friends, she could wear the dress then. She'll be fine."

"Think so?"

"I do." Darla peered into her eyes. "That's not all, is it? What else has you so upset?"

"It's Trevor," Isabel said. And now that she'd gotten to her deepest concern, she felt her eyes fill. "He's…disappointed, I guess is the word. In me."

"Because he kissed you, and Angie saw it?"

"Because I didn't tell him I had hopes of marrying Roger, or that everyone at home knew about my wishes."

"Do you still have those hopes?"

"No."

"Then you told Trevor the truth. Maybe before you even knew it was the truth."

Darla might be right.

But Isabel still had a problem. She frowned. "Trevor's so intense. We got really close. We trusted each other. I think I blew it."

"He's intense when he cares." Darla pulled a tissue from the box in front of her and handed it across. "You've got muddy tear tracks."

After Isabel had wiped them away, Darla said. "Anyway, don't worry. We'll find a way to make that stubborn cuss listen."

TREVOR KNELT IN FRONT of little Angie Corbett in a Denver airport terminal, peering into her eyes. "You'll send pictures?" he asked. "I could use some for my fridge. My youngest sister is two, and she can only scribble."

"What do you want me to draw?" Angie appeared quite serious about filling this request.

"Pigs or chickens?"

"I'll draw you some pigs," Angie promised. "But you probly don't have crayons, to draw something for me."

"I'll send you postcards."

"What's a pose-card?"

"It's a card with one side blank, so I can write you a note, and one side filled with a photograph—a picture."

"A pit-tcher of what?"

"Of anything. I'll find you one with mountains on it, or maybe a hummingbird."

"I like black bears better."

"Then black bears it is."

She frowned, as if considering the fairness of their intended trade. Then she gave a satisfied nod. "Okay. Send me a pose-card. Bye, Mr. Trebor."

He stuck his hand out to shake hers, but she only frowned at it. By six most children wouldn't have learned to shake hands, would they?

"Put this hand in mine," he coached, touching the palm of her right hand. When she'd done so, he shook her hand and then surprised himself by pulling her forward to hug her. "Goodbye, Miss Angie. It was nice meeting you."

He felt her nod against his ear.

When he backed away and stood up, Isabel was right there. Trevor watched her crouch down to say something to the child. He turned to walk to the nearby chairs and sat down to wait.

He didn't want to hear their goodbye. He'd only driven the pair to the airport because Darla had twisted his arm.

He knew he was cranky. He thought he had a right to be, and he was absolutely certain this way was best. Isabel could go home and face Roger with a clear conscience.

A flight attendant approached Isabel and Angie, then the first boarding calls came over the loudspeaker. Trevor glanced at the little pink backpack in the chair beside him. He gathered the papers the little girl had strewn around, and one of them caught his attention. The crayoned figure was clearly identifiable. It was green, with an oversize half-circle smile. Angie had drawn a bright red heart, quite large, on the chest.

With a fat, black zigzag dissecting its middle.

The figure next to the Grinch, with long brown hair and a heart with a similar zigzag, had to be Isabel.

The little girl might want Isabel as a stepmother, but she knew something different, didn't she?

Trevor stuffed the papers inside the zippered compartment, closed it and carried the bundle to where Isabel was saying a last goodbye.

Angie shrugged into it, then took the attendant's hand before peering at Trevor one more time. "You won't forget I like bear pose-cards?"

"I won't."

Then she peered at Isabel. "An' when you get home, we'll have a pah-ty with cake an' balloons an' my purple dress?"

"That's right."

"'Kay."

Isabel's face was chalk-white as her sidekick disappeared into the corridor with the attendant.

He'd been biting his tongue for hours, but sharp words came spilling out. "You'll see her in a week."

Isabel gave him a funny look, and he shut up again.

After the plane had vanished, they started for the Burch Lodge in his Jeep. He turned on the radio, the dial set to classic rock, and cranked up the volume.

After three or four miles and half a song, Isabel turned down the volume. "Are you going to give me the silent treatment all the way back?" she asked.

"You have something to talk about?"

"Trevor, this is very hard for me, you know."

"Angie will be there when you get home, Isabel." He spoke more patiently this time.

"I know she will. But I feel as if it's my fault that she's leaving. If I'd been totally honest with you, we wouldn't have done what we did, and she wouldn't have seen us. And she wouldn't be going home."

Trevor wasn't so sure. He'd known Roger was a recent ex, and that hadn't mattered. And he'd always known that Isabel wanted the fairy tale. Marriage. Kids. All the things he'd rejected.

He simply hadn't known whom she might marry, specifically. Why would knowing a name make him so mad?

"You really thought you wanted to marry Roger?"

She shrugged. "He fits my life."

"Guess he would."

"I didn't know there should be more between us," Isabel said. She looked across at Trevor. "You want to know something funny?"

"I don't have a very good sense of humor right now."

"I noticed."

Despite himself, he smiled.

"I came out here thinking I could make Roger miss me, right? I didn't ask *him* if we were headed for marriage. I waited for him to propose."

"You're an old-fashioned girl, that way."

"No, I'm not. Think about it. With you I'd have asked. We're connected. I say what I think, and expect you to do the same."

He frowned as he stopped for a light. "Well, I guess that's right. You're pretty direct with me."

"I've never been so at ease with Roger."

That had sounded like an honest admission, and it

eased Trevor's mood. No matter how many times he tried to distance himself from Isabel, she kept yanking him close again.

Except he still needed to know something.

"Were you in love with Roger?" he asked, watching her face as he waited for the light to change.

Isabel pointed at the light, and he drove through the intersection. It was a moment before she answered, "I thought he was the kind of man I *should* love. Mom insisted that men were fickle. I found a man who was steadfast. She said they were lazy. I found a hard worker."

Trevor raised his eyebrows.

"If Roger dropped to his knee the moment he saw me at home, I'd be upset," Isabel said. "Not happy."

"Thank you for telling me that," he said.

It would be foolish to say more. She'd be going home soon to deal with steadfast, hardworking Roger.

After a moment Isabel turned up the radio again, and they finished the drive in silence.

When he pulled into the lodge parking lot, Trevor turned off the ignition and sat staring at the front of the building. "I'm headed home," he said. "My bags are in the back, and I finished tying up loose ends here after the campers and counselors left yesterday."

"Of course." Isabel's voice was overly polite.

He'd intended to wave to her and leave. He'd see her at the wedding next weekend, anyway, and he had plenty to do. But sometime during the drive, he'd changed his mind.

"It might be smart to check the cabins for personal

items, though." He neglected to mention it to Isabel, but the campers and counselors had done that task, twice. "I might swing by this evening, to look around."

"Good idea," she said, her blue eyes serious.

"If you're around, you can help me."

"Trevor, I could check and call you if I find anything."

"It's a short drive and no trouble at all," he said. "And...maybe afterward we could go to dinner. Sam and Darla deserve an evening alone, don't you think?"

"What a great idea!"

The warmth in her smile could melt every snowcap in these Rockies. But even if Trevor knew it would do exactly that, he'd try to coax it out of her again.

Chapter Twelve

"Hello, Callie? It's Isabel. Guess you aren't home. Things are…okay, here. I wanted to talk for a minute. But, well, shoot." She sighed. "I'll talk to you soon, 'kay?"

She started to hang up, then jerked the phone back to her mouth. "Don't worry. I'm fine."

After returning the receiver to its cradle, she sat at the edge of the Ripple River bed and sighed again.

Cautious Callie had found something lasting with Ethan. She might have been able to help Isabel think through her questions.

How did a person know if her feelings for someone were more than attraction or curiosity?

Scratch that. Isabel knew. What she didn't know was how to handle it. Did she tell Trevor? How?

Isabel glanced at the clock and tried not to panic. Trevor had called her three times today. Once, they'd spoken about where she'd like to go for dinner tonight. A half hour later he'd phoned to say that he'd heard Sam and Darla wouldn't be at home tonight after all. They were heading to Greeley to help Darla's mother choose a mother-of-the-bride dress, then they would bring her back to the ranch.

Since Trevor's stated reason for going was to give Sam and Darla a night alone, he'd wondered if Isabel still wanted to go. She'd said yes, of course. Then he'd said okay and he'd hung up. Moments ago he'd called again to say he was on his way.

With twenty minutes to spare, she was dressed and ready and the butterflies were loose again. Isabel yanked the receiver to her ear and dialed her own Augusta number.

"Yo, this is Josie."

"Hi, it's me."

"Hey!" her sister said. "Have you seen the e-mail I sent you a while ago?"

"No. What was in it?"

"You got an order for some baskets. I went ahead and gave the buyer a delivery date, since you'll be home soon. And the woman who bought the baby quilt called to say she loved it. She wants three more for her pregnant nieces."

"Good," Isabel said, grateful to know she'd be very busy at home for a while.

"I noticed Angie in her yard when I drove past earlier," Josie said. "She's back before you, huh? I'm glad you finally insisted on some time to yourself."

"Roger *asked* me to send Angie home. I didn't insist."

"Whatever," Josie said, unconcerned, as usual, with other people's motives. "What's up?"

"Ever been in love?"

"What kind of question is that?"

"A serious one. Things are happening here."

Her sister hooted. "It's that professor again, isn't it? He's being decent, then?"

"Guess you could say that."

"Oh, good. You needed a summer fling."

Did she and Trevor qualify as a fling? She thought about him every moment, and had begun to dream of babies with greenish gray eyes.

Life had been simpler before this trip. Her dream babies had had Roger's brown eyes and siblings Isabel already loved. Her dream life had been in Kansas, near her beloved nephew, Luke, her brother-in-law, Ethan, and her two best friends, Callie and Josie.

She kept wishing Darla's wedding day wouldn't arrive. A selfish wish, surely.

"I've seen you get involved with lots of guys," Isabel told Josie now. "You have fun and say goodbye. Don't you ever fall for one?"

"Come *on*. In love? Hardly."

"How do you avoid it?"

Josie gasped. "Whoa! Are you serious about this guy?"

"What's serious?"

"Okay, back up. Have you slept with him?"

Lord, she wanted to. In about sixteen minutes. "No. But we've gone beyond kissing."

"Do you *want* to sleep with him?"

In fifteen minutes and forty-eight seconds. "Think I should?"

Her sister chuckled, which was good because it knocked some of the seriousness out of the idea.

"If you want to, big sis," she said. "But here are a few ground rules. If you go to bed with him, remember that those three little words don't mean anything if either of you is naked or touching the bed."

Josie made it all sound fun. Manageable.

"Lust can fool you," Josie warned. "Happens to everyone."

"Oh."

"Don't *you* say those words either. You hear me, Isabel? Think about everything Mother told us about men."

Ella Blume couldn't have known much about men or romantic love. Isabel had felt something akin to love several times today. When Trevor had hugged Angie at the terminal gate, she'd felt proud of him. When he'd warmed up to Isabel on the drive home, she'd respected his fair-mindedness. When he'd asked her out for tonight, she'd been excited. Every time, she'd heard a whisper in her soul that said her deep feelings for him would never falter.

"Say something, big sis," Josie prompted. "Say, 'I won't profess my undying love to a guy I'll be leaving in a week.' Promise you won't."

Isabel knew what Josie was telling her. She would return home soon, so why create problems? Except that she wanted Trevor to know that he'd meant something to her. "I can't promise."

"Then at least let him say it first, somewhere in public when you aren't naked. That's the only way to know if a guy means it. You know they think with their Johnsons."

"Josie!"

"Sorry. I'm around guys a lot," Josie said. "If he says it in a believable place, call me. I'll talk you through it."

"Sounds like an intervention."

"Oh, it is, sweetums."

Isabel glanced at the clock. She had only minutes left before Trevor's arrival. If she hung up, she'd get nervous again. She stalled. "How are you, Jo? Any news?"

"Got a new guy," Josie answered. "He's so cute—a finish carpenter who can actually swing dance. He has great big puppy-dog eyes, and he brought me flowers last night."

"I thought you didn't like to get flowers."

"I don't—too many expectations. But at least this guy only brought irises."

"Irises don't imply expectations?"

"Not really. Maybe that he wants a roll in the garden." Josie laughed at her own joke. "Anyway, I think he cut these from plants in his sister's yard."

Isabel listened as her sister continued talking about her date last night. After they hung up, she stepped across to the mirror to check her hair one last time. When she heard the doorbell, every one of those butterflies danced. Something lively. Maybe a swing dance.

She left the bedroom and jogged down the hall to the front door to greet Trevor, telling him that Sam and Darla had already left for Greeley.

Later, Isabel would try to remember if he had responded to her greeting. He'd had a grin and a bouquet of sunflowers. "Kansas flowers for a Kansas girl," he'd said, while Isabel considered calling Josie again, to ask about their meaning.

And he'd stepped inside before she'd invited him in.

He pressed the thick stems into her hand and kissed her, right there in the foyer. His ready desire made Isabel feel good. Sexy. Pretty. Wanted. She returned the compliment by looping her empty hand around his neck and shoving the door closed behind him with her foot.

She should at least put the flowers in water, she thought even while she kissed.

But Trevor's hands had moved to the small of her back, tugging her close. His kiss deepened, then she felt his arousal and forgot the flowers until she tried to slide her hands up his chest. The stems were heavy and cumbersome.

She dropped the flowers onto the nearest chair and focused. She undid a button on his shirt and slipped her finger inside the opening. Pulling her lips from his, she said, "I've wanted to touch you here ever since the first time I saw your chest."

"You have touched me there."

"I want to do it again."

He unfastened a single button of her gingham jacket and slipped a finger inside, caressing her breast above her lacy bra. "I've wanted to touch you here," he murmured, his voice husky.

"You have."

"I want to do it again."

Funny, how neither of them laughed at their jokes. She kissed him as she unbuttoned another small white button, making an opening large enough for her hand.

She kissed him as she felt him work more of the black buttons loose, until he could lay her jacket open.

She might have been disappointed when he broke the kiss to gaze at her, except she loved the heat in his eyes. And she adored that devilish look when he moved his thumbs across her lace-clad breasts.

She grabbed his hands and tugged him backward, toward the hall that led to the guest bedroom she now had to herself. She wanted to be in his arms, naked.

They slowed in the entry to the hallway, where a shared smile started a whole new series of kisses, but neither of them stopped moving toward that bed.

Trevor closed the bedroom door behind them. They were alone in the house, but Isabel knew why he'd shut them inside. Even if Darla and Sam found cause to turn around and return home, they wouldn't knock on a closed door.

No one would need to rush around dressing or stop or regret a single moment of this special night.

Trevor's intense expression was heartbreakingly sexy as he finished unbuttoning his shirt. He shrugged out of it, then raised an eyebrow and dropped his gaze to her open jacket—an "I dare you" look if Isabel had ever seen one. She slipped out of her jacket.

Trevor unbuckled his belt; Isabel unfastened her bra.

He yanked off his shoes; she slid out of her sandals.

After he'd dropped his socks on the floor, he broke the pattern. "You sure you're okay with this?" he asked.

Isabel wasn't Josie-bold, but this evening was part of her memory bank and she wouldn't ruin it with false modesty. She wanted to see him. Wanted him to see her. Wanted the entire experience to be red-hot and unforgettable.

"More than okay," she said, glancing toward his pants.

The fire in his eyes was enough to cause a sharp spasm of want to surprise Isabel. He slid off his pants, tossed them to the side and without even waiting for his next turn, removed his boxer shorts, too.

He was gorgeous. Ridged and smooth and ready.

She stepped toward him as she removed her skirt.

Met him as she began to slide her panties downward.

Kissed him with everything she had as they fell naked onto the bed.

He gripped her hands, pulling them above her head as he settled his body atop hers. She expected him to push inside her immediately, but he rested his hardness between her thighs, then kissed down her neck to her breasts. The sensation of his kisses was intense.

Her body felt like a party.

Her desire grew to a deep, hard want.

She knew what Josie had meant when she'd said lust could fool a person. Trevor's hands and eyes and mouth made her feel so good and desired, turning that whispery feeling into a shout.

She felt so loved.

He returned his mouth to hers in an openmouthed, hungry kiss, then abruptly he left her. He rolled right off her and the bed, and bent down to pick up his pants.

He pulled a packet from a pocket and took care of protection.

He returned his hot body to hers and pushed inside her, filling her so perfectly she didn't want him to move, ever.

This felt like love.

But he did move.

She did, too, slowing and quickening and deepening her movements alongside him, searching for that high feeling she'd never quite captured before.

She was almost there, she thought.

A tingling. A reaching—almost.

Oh! He kissed her breasts again. And looked at them and ran his hands to her waist and gazed into her eyes.

"Relax, Isabel." He trailed his hands along her tummy, brushing his fingers against her curls. Then he moved them deeper. Touching her.

She forgot to try.

"Let go, baby," he whispered. "I love you."

He deepened and slowed his movements, urgency evident on his furrowed brow, until he let out a long, low moan and Isabel felt herself soar and soar and soar.

She'd had ideas about what she'd been missing. She couldn't have imagined this.

She made love to Trevor four times that night. In between sessions, they put the sunflowers into water and scrounged dinner from the kitchen and laughed about everything from Angie's Grinch drawings to dumb, traded jokes.

Isabel was glad she had spoken to Josie rather than Callie this evening. She might have taken his impassioned words seriously. As in, "I love you forever, in and out of bed." As in, "Let's do something about this six-hundred-mile separation between your house and mine."

But a man who hated weddings because he didn't believe in forever relationships wouldn't be asking for forever. He'd been saying that she pleased him there in bed and for the moment.

Perhaps everyone had been wrong. Perhaps Isabel wasn't destined for motherhood and marriage. Perhaps she was meant to become a mysterious spinster who got a faraway look in her eyes when she remembered that certain man from her youth.

Maybe the memories would be enough.

HE MANAGED FOUR DAYS. When he finally dialed the number for the Burch Lodge, he got Darla and asked for Sam.

"You checked your messages, bud?" Sam asked, his voice terse.

"Why do you think I'm calling?"

"Lord only knows, Trevor. I started thinking you'd been abducted on your way home the other night."

Trevor stared out the screened window of his back porch. "I was busy."

"Your house slide down the damn hill?"

"No." At Sam's silence, Trevor added, "You know I have catch-up to do after the camp weeks. The real world beckons."

"I think you left a part of your world here, and she's pretty upset."

Ah! But that was the problem, wasn't it? Isabel wasn't a part of his world. "She talk to you and Darla?" Trevor asked, wishing he could ask about her but thinking he had no right. No reason that made sense.

"She didn't have to," Sam said. "It's pretty obvious this is tough for her."

It was tough for Trevor, too. And he'd been the one to confess true feelings. Not her.

He didn't even know what he wanted, or why he woke up every day feeling madder than a bear within claws' reach of a tree-hung food pack. Would a promise that she'd send a damn Christmas card every year help? Another wild night or two?

"Yeah, well. What would you suggest I do, Sam?"

"Talk to her."

"All the talk in the world won't change the circumstances. She's on her way home."

"You should've thought of that before."

Sam wasn't usually this slow. Trevor *had* thought of this before, right at the start, and he'd been raked over the coals for being rude. "She there?" he asked.

"Yeeaah." Sam's tone said, "And what of it? If you talk to her, you say the right things."

Protecting her again.

What right things, though?

Hi, babe. I still love you. Do you want to get together tonight and make me love you more, so I'll be more upset when you go home?

"Never mind," he said to Sam. "I called to see if there's anything you need for Saturday."

"Saturday."

"Mmm-hmm."

"You mean my wedding day?"

Trevor nearly clicked off the phone. He didn't need Sam's harassment. "That's what I mean."

"You can't hurt yourself by saying the word, you know."

"Just answer the damn question. What do you need, when and where?"

"That's not my department," Sam said. "Hold on."

Sam murmured something, and Darla came on the line instantly. Which meant she must have been standing there listening to every word.

Isabel could be there, too. Trevor wondered if she was. How she'd been. If their night together had messed up her head as much as it had his.

"I'm glad you asked to help, Trevor," Darla said. "We're getting down to the wire, here."

No kidding.

"Of course we're keeping things low-key, but we could use a favor."

"What is it?"

"Our dresses and suits are at Lynn's Boutique, there in Boulder. You know the place?"

"My mother used Lynn's for two of her weddings," he said. "I know it."

"Could you be a dear and pick up our things?"

Good. An easy job, and he'd fulfill part of his duty as best man. He'd never forgotten Isabel's disbelief that he could be so cynical about his best friend's wedding. "Sure I can," he said. "In fact, I can leave in a few minutes."

"Wonderful! Isabel will be waiting at the lodge for you, say, in about a hour?"

She expected him to take Isabel? "Darla, what?"

"She'll have the receipt, and she may need to have someone at Lynn's adjust her headpiece. You have time to wait?"

"You want me to come get Isabel?" Dumb question, he knew. But he'd told himself he'd see Isabel twice more. At the wedding rehearsal dinner and at the wedding. He'd told himself they'd be smart to cut things off now, before any more damage was done.

This idea was senseless.

He lived just outside Boulder. He'd be driving all the way to the lodge, getting Isabel and returning to his home city, then looping back around.

This was just...more love matching.

"I know what you're doing, Darla," he said.

"What?" Her voice was high, innocent. "Making sure that your best friend and I have a wonderful wedding experience?"

Again Trevor considered clicking off the phone. Maybe he could pack up and go on a month-long hike, until the wedding was over and Isabel was gone.

He wanted to see her. He knew weddings, and he knew as the main attendants he and Isabel would be busy. Perhaps one more private meeting would be good. He could say a better goodbye and try not to leap on her in the doorway as he had the other night.

He'd stay in public. Keep things friendly but sane.

"I'll be there within an hour," he said.

He drove fast and arrived in forty-three minutes.

Isabel met him outside the lodge, purse tucked under her elbow and eyes full of emotion. She came out to the Jeep and slid into the passenger side before he'd figured out what to say to her in greeting.

Something like, *Sorry I didn't call you. I realized I was in love*.

She made the greeting easy. Smiled. Said, "Hi, Trevor."

"Hi."

"You okay?"

Are you kidding?

"Fine. Busy." He started the Jeep and backed out, then headed south toward Boulder. "Isabel, the other night was incredible," he said after a moment. "I didn't mean to—"

"Shh."

Trevor kept his eyes on the winding road. "I meant to say I'm sorry."

"We both wanted the other night, and I thought it was incredible, too. Don't *apologize*."

He glanced her way, met that blue-eyed gaze. "I'm not apologizing for what happened. Only for what happened afterward." He shrugged. "I left. I didn't call."

"I don't think I expected you to, really," Isabel said. "We could have tried to claim every possible second, but that might make things harder in the long run."

This time he held her gaze for a moment. "You're pretty amazing, do you know that?"

She blinked at him, her eyes troubled, then turned forward in her seat. "I'm just trying to find the best way to deal with a tough situation."

Exactly his thoughts.

Exactly his feelings.

But he'd missed out on knowing, and he wanted to know: had their relationship affected her as much as it had him? Though he'd dated his other girlfriends for much longer, he remembered them with an idle fondness. He couldn't imagine looking back at his brief time with Isabel without missing her fiercely.

They drove in thick silence, and soon they passed the place on the highway where they'd met. Though the landscape was similar for a long stretch, Trevor had memorized the shape of the rocks and the break in the trees just beyond where they'd stood.

He wondered if Isabel knew where they were.

"There it is," she murmured. "Would you have dreamed all that could happen in only seven weeks?"

"Eight." He knew it was eight, because he'd counted the days on his calendar.

"Seven from that first day to the other night," she said. "Eight to the wedding."

Right. He'd counted the days until her departure, hadn't he? She must be thinking of their night together as the end.

As he should.

"I thought that guy on the highway was so exciting," she said. "Vital. Gentlemanly. A sexy man living a grand life in a grand place."

He glanced at her, frowning. "Change your mind?"

"On the contrary."

"I haven't always been a gentleman, though, have I?"

"How would my mentioning that help?"

Isabel was generous, Trevor thought. "I am living a good life, I think," he said. "It's always kept me happy."

Before, he thought, but he bit his tongue. And because he felt her looking at him, he added, "I thought you were hot."

"You thought I was an idiot."

"No. Just…gullible. I could tell you had no clue about how sexy you were, standing there in your short skirt and long legs, offering a wide-open smile to a man you'd just met."

She frowned. "I might have been gullible, but I… well, I had a good feeling about you, right off the bat."

"You didn't know me, though."

"Maybe not. My hunch was right."

He was glad she thought so.

His hunch had been right, too. He'd known he was attracted. Definitely in lust at first sight. And intrigued by her small-town charm. He'd known, after he learned Isabel's identity, that he should maintain a distance.

But he hadn't.

And she'd wrecked his heart in seven weeks.

They arrived at the shop, and Trevor loitered in the doorway while Isabel spoke to the clerk. The two women worked with the delicate headpiece, adjusting the fit, but the entire transaction took less than ten minutes.

Then Trevor was striding toward the Jeep with his arms full of suits and thinking he wasn't ready to return Isabel to the lodge.

He was much more inclined to kidnap her. He could take her along on his month-long escape. Maybe after a month he'd be able to breathe when he thought about her leaving.

They loaded the Jeep and took their seats, and Trevor stuck his keys in the ignition.

He toyed with them. After a moment he turned to peer at Isabel. "Look at that! We're sitting in front of the very store that makes the best pie in the U.S.A." He nodded toward the glass-front bakery with that very claim printed in white lettering across the door.

She turned her head to look, then gazed at him again. "Wow. Guess you Boulder folks are lucky."

He nodded. Their teasing couldn't lighten his mood.

"Actually, Angie told me that the cherry pie is very good," Isabel said. "She had hers à la mode."

Trevor's gaze probed hers. "Want to get coffee, test this claim for ourselves?" He paused. "Talk somewhere besides the Jeep?"

She smiled brilliantly, and he responded in kind.

They weren't supposed to do that.

So they got out of Trevor's Jeep and went into the shop to order pie and coffee.

Although the cherry pie was excellent, neither of them ate much. They sat across from each other at a small round table in a brightly lit, modestly decorated room, sipping coffee from red ceramic mugs and talking about Saturday's wedding.

Darla and Sam had written simple vows and invited fewer than thirty people. Trevor and Isabel agreed that their friends were doing things right.

They talked about Isabel's business—she had orders awaiting her at home. They talked about Trevor's preparations for the upcoming school session, and his efforts to organize his house after his six-week stint up at the camp.

He said nothing that was on his mind.

He didn't ask his questions.

Did she love him?

Would she entertain thoughts of staying in touch?

Of *staying?*

After they'd finished their second cups of coffee, Trevor grew tired of hunting down safe topics.

He eyed Isabel. "Ready to go, then?"

She stared at him. "To the lodge?"

He shrugged, his thoughts unfocused. "Or somewhere else, if you have any ideas."

He wanted more. He couldn't ask.

Isabel would leave after the wedding, and for the life of him, Trevor couldn't think of a way to say goodbye to her in any way that would honor their relationship.

Or satisfy him.

Chapter Thirteen

Isabel peered at Trevor, wishing she knew how to fix this. How to make both of them feel better. She reached across the table and ran her index finger along his forehead frown. When she lifted her hand away, his scowl was even fiercer.

And apparently he was waiting for her to decide.

Where to go?

Callie would tell her to return to the lodge. Anything else would prolong the pain.

Josie would advise her to savor every experience.

"I hope you're suggesting that we go to your place," Isabel said, because at this moment Josie's way sounded the least painful. "Because I'd love to see it."

Had that frown grown fiercer?

"My place," he said. "Uh. Guess we are close. And we have time." He sighed, shaking his head. Staring at her. Still frowning.

The man was too intense. That was what Josie would say.

Isabel wondered if all of his breakups were this traumatic.

"Think we can handle it all right?" he asked. "Being alone, I mean. I *do* live alone."

Isabel's cheeks grew hot. She felt brazen again. "Oh! Well, I didn't mean—" She had no clue what to say. She *had* meant to suggest everything he was probably thinking.

Making love one more night with a man who made her feel.

"Actually, that's a good idea," he said, his forehead clearing. "But we should plan to *do* something."

With a narrow-eyed gaze, he stared out the bakery window, considering. "Want to make dinner together?" he asked. "We'd have to decide what to make, and go by the grocery store."

That sounded like something dedicated lovers would do. Did he know? "Sounds perfect."

They telephoned the lodge to tell Darla and Sam about their plans, and an hour later Isabel stood in Trevor's entry hall, holding a watermelon. He was right behind her, carrying two grocery bags.

"Go on in." He strode around her and led her through a living room with oversize furniture that made the large room look cozy. "I'd better get these eggs in the fridge," he said when she paused to look around. "And you can set that melon in the sink."

She followed him into a surprisingly well-equipped kitchen—all clean white walls and shiny chrome appliances—and rid herself of the cumbersome melon.

"I'm starving. How 'bout you?" Trevor yanked a couple of cans from his bag, stacking them near the stove.

They'd each rejected the U.S.A.'s best cherry pie, not

too long ago. She wasn't hungry. Isabel had hoped to see his house first. Maybe try to talk more. "You want to cook and eat now?" she asked.

"That was the idea, right?" The dear man glanced at her, looking as if he might jump a mile if she said boo, then returned to his grocery unpacking.

Some of Isabel's best memories revolved around her kitchen at home. Some of the most relaxed times. Kitchens made people chatter and relax. "Okay. We'll cook and eat now," she said, eyeing the full sink. "Where's your bathroom? I need to wash up."

He turned around, his hands full of lemons.

"Never mind, I'll find it."

She trooped back through his living room, admiring the oversize wood stove, then made her way into a wide, arched hallway that was papered in the same cumin-and-paprika-colored pattern as the living room.

When she passed a huge room that must be Trevor's—the first open door down the hall—she peered inside. A king-size bed beckoned, its red silk sheets exposed to her prying eyes.

She could imagine him there, strong legs tangled in those sheets.

She could imagine both of them there.

She scurried past. Her thoughts might put the two of them in that bed, but she couldn't be that brazen. Judging from Trevor's serious mood, he might refuse her.

She continued along, searching for the bathroom.

"You okay, Isabel?" he called.

"I'll be right there!"

She found the bathroom at the end of his hallway and stepped inside. The room was about as big as her bedroom at home. She'd just turned to see a gleaming gray tub when she heard Trevor's footsteps. He had followed her down the hall.

"You have a hot tub in here?" she asked.

"I'm a runner and climber," he said as he stepped inside. "There's nothing better than a hot soak when your muscles are tired."

She turned to look at him, realizing that the space wasn't so large. Not with both of them sharing it, surely thinking about all the incredible sex they could have had but wouldn't.

"Ever been in a hot tub?" he asked.

"Nope." She shrugged. "One more thing I haven't done." This conversation couldn't be casual, but Isabel tried. She turned to approach the sink on another wall, but he caught her wrist.

"What the hell, want to try it?"

She turned, eyes seeking his, and his kiss saved her from answering. Somehow he managed to keep his lips attached to hers while he reached around to open the taps. Moments later they discarded their clothing and plunged into the tub.

Before they went far enough for it to matter, Trevor said, "Condoms aren't really an option in a hot tub."

Of course Isabel moved away from him, but he pulled her back into his arms. "We can do other things."

Isabel explored and tasted, experiencing several firsts, and wondered if this evening would forever rate in her memory as her most erotic. She knew the thoughts would always make her feel wickedly sexy, even if she was alive at ninety-nine.

Later Trevor helped Isabel out of the tub and handed her a towel. Dressing alongside him felt right. They talked and handed each other clothing items and soon returned to the kitchen for that dinner and conversation.

Trevor looked loose-limbed. Isabel felt…grown-up, as if she'd finally stepped out of childhood and into the richness of adult life.

She'd do it all again, even knowing it had to end.

He scooped mayonnaise and Dijon mustard into a bowl while Isabel stood next to him, reading the recipe they were following. She opened a drawer, then shut it and tried another. Finally she peered across at him. "Measuring spoons?"

"Don't own any," he said.

She reopened the first drawer, pulling out a regular tablespoon. As she measured herbs and spices into the same bowl, she said, "I like your house, Trevor."

"Thanks." He sliced a scallion and dumped in the pieces, then she opened a can of salmon and flaked the usable pieces inside.

He added egg; she crumbed and added crackers.

"Butter?" she asked.

"In the fridge door."

She located the package and brought it across while he formed patties. As she located a pan and heated the butter, she wondered if he'd noticed how well they worked together.

Or did all of his lady friends benefit from his willingness to work in a kitchen? Isabel didn't like thinking about Trevor with other women, but that's where they were headed, wasn't it?

A life of abstinence, or other people.

As he nestled the patties inside the sizzling pan, he asked, "Do you think sometimes people can be so attuned to each other that they fall in love fast, and stay in love?"

Had the unbeliever learned something from her, too? Isabel hoped so. "Sometimes," she said. "My older sister married her first love, and they'll celebrate their eleventh anniversary this year."

"Wow."

"Callie and Ethan make commitment look worth it," she said. "If it weren't for them, I'm not sure I'd have even dated Roger."

Why had she mentioned that name? She didn't want to spoil the mood. But Trevor turned over a salmon cake, seemingly unaffected, and a wonderful smell permeated the room.

"I love being around you," he said as he flipped patties.

"Thanks. I think we get along."

"I'm in love with you, you know."

Isabel glanced at his shirt, his pants. She studied his actions.

He'd said that out of bed and fully dressed.

He glanced at her, his lips tilted up. "What?"

"That was the first time you said those words with your clothes on."

She took the spatula from him and set it on the counter so she could turn him around and hug him. He felt warm and sturdy against her, and she absorbed his strength.

The words felt so big—so tough. The time since she'd met Trevor so short.

But she did love him. She did. She'd remember him as the first man she truly loved. Maybe the only one.

"I love you, too," she finally said against his ear.

"You do?"

She gave him a long kiss that said so.

When she backed up, Trevor eyed her with a frown. "So what do we do about it?"

Do?

Oh. He was bringing up *that* question. The question they'd talked about and hadn't been able to answer.

What did they do? Well, they got on with their lives.

He'd ended relationships before, presumably more than once. She had never even settled things with Roger.

One of the salmon cakes popped.

Isabel peered at Trevor, who didn't react. She turned to pick up the spatula but simply held it. "I don't know," she said. "You always hear of spinsters who never married because they had a passionate affair in their youth. I suppose I thought I'd be one of them."

"You intend to become a spinster?"

"I don't know. But I know I'll never forget you."

"Am I insane to think you might stay here?"

Smoke curled out of the pan. Trevor swore and pulled the cakes off the burner just as the smell of scorched fish reached Isabel's nostrils. She turned over the cakes. The bottoms were very brown.

"Plates?" she asked.

He opened a cabinet and pulled out two, and she concentrated on dividing the salmon cakes while he turned off the burner.

She put the spatula down and stood scowling at it. "I need to get this clear. You're asking me to move here to Colorado, to hang around. To *date*."

Out of the corner of her eye, she saw him shift his weight. "Yes."

Now she turned to look at him. "I don't know, Trevor. I work from a house that is designed for my business, and I lead a full life. I never thought I'd even consider moving for a…a boyfriend. It sounds impulsive, and I'm twenty-seven years old. I'd like to be a mother, someday."

His eyes were dark with questions. "So this is really it, then?"

"We talked about this, Trevor." She spoke softly, soothing him even while she craved comfort for herself. "This has to be it."

Both of them turned to stare at the salmon cakes. They had bags of chips and jars of pickles waiting on the table.

They had soda in the fridge and a melon in the sink.

Isabel left the kitchen. She might have headed for Trevor's Jeep, but he followed her and grabbed her hand.

"Stay awhile."

She frowned.

"One evening, Isabel. Stay with me one evening. I'll take you home later, but tomorrow's night's the rehearsal dinner. After that …" He turned his palms up, raised his brows.

Hadn't she already decided to experience what she could? "I know," she said. "Okay. For a while. But let's drop the subject of what comes next."

The room filled with silence as he looked at her, not sharing what he was thinking.

A heaviness settled in Isabel's stomach. "We could destroy what time we do have left," she said.

"Okay." One corner of his mouth rose, but his gaze was sober. "Want to go back in and try to eat?"

She shook her head, tears of regret pricking at her eyes. "I'm not hungry."

He nodded, paused to consider again. "Want to go out? I could show you some of my favorite places here in Boulder."

Maybe if she were in a different mood. Everything had changed. Trevor wanted something from her she couldn't give. He'd wanted it enough to ask her for it, and she'd had to refuse him.

She wondered if she would always regret her choice.

"Maybe I should just go, Trevor," she said. "Things are…different already."

He took her hand. "I have an idea." He led her to the kitchen again, and on through to a small laundry room. He opened a door and stepped out onto a raised, screened-in porch. He waved toward a set of wicker chairs that faced a small yard and a forested slope beyond.

"This is gorgeous, Trevor."

"Sit. I'll get us some wine."

While she waited, Isabel convinced herself that she could handle tonight. She'd grown up a lot in the past few weeks, and she felt braver. Bolder. She wouldn't regret this time.

Trevor returned with two glasses of chardonnay and sat in the love seat beside her. They wandered into his bedroom an hour later. Trevor kissed her, his mood somber but loving, and she rushed him into the bed.

Into sex.

Maybe she was hoping she could forget their goodbye, but it loomed even larger in her thoughts. She started crying after the first few, urgent moments. "I'm sorry," she said, frustrated with herself. "I can't. This is just too difficult."

He rolled away from her.

"Could you take me back to the lodge now?"

"If that's what you want."

His wording didn't escape her notice.

After they dressed, Isabel grabbed her purse and Trevor led her out to the Jeep. He started the drive to the lodge at nine o'clock. On the way Isabel tried to explain that they could call each other and exchange e-mails.

He nodded, but she knew he would never write. It wouldn't be enough, just as their last lovemaking attempt hadn't been.

You couldn't get your fill of someone you loved.

But Trevor would get over her, she knew. He'd committed himself to a single life, so he must have made this same choice before.

And she, well, she'd come to Colorado to help her dear friend plan a wedding. She'd done so much more.

She'd learned so much.

She couldn't settle for a steady, hardworking man just because he didn't fit her mother's beliefs about men. If she ever fell in love again, she knew what she wanted. She wanted more—a man like Trevor without the commitment issues. A relationship like the one they'd found, with a marriage certificate.

For now she'd focus on Darla and the wedding.

And then she was headed home.

SAM AND DARLA'S tall, gentle-eyed minister had been very patient, waiting out under the gazebo for twenty-two minutes before Sam's cell phone rang. Before he'd walked away to carry on a private conversation, Sam had caught Darla's eye and murmured, "Maybe it's Trevor."

No one had heard from him all day. Sam and Darla had commented on his absence several times as they'd worked around the property, preparing for tomorrow's big day.

Isabel thought he was just recovering, gathering his wits before he arrived to the rehearsal dinner tonight.

Isabel had kept busy. While she'd washed plates and utensils with Darla's mother, Isabel had talked to the older woman about her prognosis. Georgia looked good. She wore a wig very like her own hair, and she claimed to enjoy her recent weight loss. Isabel could see that Darla got some of her energy from her mother. She suspected that they'd both be fine.

Isabel had also tied bows to the backs of two dozen folding chairs, and she'd accompanied Sam's father to the liquor store in Lyons, helping him pick up several cases of wine and beer.

She'd been glad for the constant work.

Now she watched Sam, standing out near the aspens and frowning as he spoke. After a couple of nods, he clicked off the phone, stuck it in his shirt pocket and strode back to the gazebo.

"Trevor's on his way," Sam said. "He says to go ahead, that he knows this routine by heart. He'll catch up with us at the restaurant if he doesn't make it here."

"Did your friend explain the holdup?" Georgia asked.

"Basically, it boils down to car trouble," Sam said. "He'll get here as soon as he can."

Sam and Darla traded a look while Isabel's relief turned into disturbance. "Does he need help?" she asked.

"He's not the one with the breakdown," Sam said. "He'll tell you about it later."

She hoped so.

The minister began explaining the sequence of events, which was fairly simple since Sam and Darla had just two attendants. Still, as Isabel concentrated on the minister's instructions, she paid as much attention to Trevor's responsibilities as to her own.

In less than a half hour they finished their run-through, and Trevor had yet to arrive. Everyone piled into cars to head down to Lyons. They were eating dinner at a small Mexican restaurant that had an outdoor seating area.

Isabel insisted on taking her own car. She'd already decided that if Trevor didn't show up, she was heading to his house to wait until he arrived. If necessary, she'd camp out on his front step until morning.

She wanted to talk to him.

Surely he wouldn't avoid the wedding because of her, would he?

Isabel arrived at the restaurant and followed the waitress outdoors, then tried to pull herself into the conversation about Sam's parents' life in Tucson. She listened and nodded and occasionally turned in her seat to check the door.

She ordered a chimichanga, ate it and listened politely, even when cars drove into the lot. Every time she thought she heard Trevor's Jeep, she watched the door.

By dessert time, she forgot to listen. She declined the great-looking fried ice cream and simply stared toward the doorway.

Surely he would come.

He arrived as everyone was finishing a cup of decaf. He walked out onto the little patio and sat down next to Isabel before anyone else had noticed him.

Isabel turned toward him, a dozen questions buzzing, but Sam's father stood to shake Trevor's hand. "Trevor Kincaid, how are you?" he said in a quiet voice much like Sam's.

"It's been a while."

They spoke like old acquaintances, and soon Sam and Darla brought out the attendants' gifts—a silver bracelet for Isabel and cuff links for Trevor. Finally the group's attention moved to Georgia, who'd begun a story about Darla's sixteenth birthday.

Isabel leaned closer to Trevor. "What happened to you?" she murmured.

"Long story," he said, glancing at her as he brought his cup of coffee to his lips.

"Someone had car trouble?" she prompted.

"A professor friend who met me on campus to discuss an article we're co-writing."

She turned in her seat to peer at him, narrowing her gaze. "This professor's car broke down in a university lot?"

Sighing, Trevor set down his coffee cup. "No-o-o. She left just before I was due to head up to the lodge, and her car stalled on her way home. She flagged me down when I passed her on the highway."

Isabel had no right to feel jealous, but she did. "You met with a female professor today?"

"Yes. It was a work-related meeting."

Isabel leaned closer, so only Trevor could hear her. "Today was awfully important to your friend Sam over there," she murmured.

Trevor bent nearer, too, and she felt his breath warm on her cheek. "I know. I didn't intend to miss it." His voice sounded low and rough, as if he was struggling for patience.

She faced forward, grabbing her cup and drinking the last few drops of coffee. It didn't help. Her throat felt tight. Her chest felt heavy. "It took two hours for you to start this professor's car?" she asked, forgetting to lower her voice.

Trevor leaned away from her and caught her gaze. "No. I *couldn't* start it," he said. "We called an auto service, and I waited with her."

Isabel blinked at him.

"Sherrilyn Averill is sixty-nine years old," Trevor said. "I couldn't just leave her on the highway."

Isabel felt her cheeks grow hot, and she peered down at her empty cup. "Of course not. Sorry."

She felt a little better. Not as good as she'd like. She wished Trevor had been with her at the Burch Lodge. She wished he'd helped her with the chairs and the liquor and the damn dishes.

She wished he'd been clinging to their every last second together. Thinking about her.

Because that was what she'd been doing, while he'd returned to an everyday world she'd never know.

"Did I miss anything important?" he asked.

"I'm sure you know you did."

"Don't worry, I know the drill."

Isabel sat back in her chair and listened to everyone chatter.

Within minutes, Sam and Darla and their families started making motions to leave.

Isabel put her hand on Trevor's arm. "Stay," she said, making sure he heard her.

Then she stood up to hug the bride. "I'll be in later," she whispered in Darla's ear. "Get a good night's sleep. I'll see you in the morning."

Darla glanced between her and Trevor, and the corners of her mouth lifted. "I'll try."

After the rest of the wedding party had left, the waitress brought her and Trevor another coffee. Isabel took a sip and then turned her chair around so she could watch his face as they talked. "Tomorrow is important to Sam and Darla," she began.

"I know."

"You won't decide to go on campus again, or take off on a morning hike?"

"No, I won't." His gaze was razor-sharp. "I might have entertained thoughts of escaping all this wedding hoopla, but I intended to be here today. Honestly."

"I know weddings aren't a lot of fun for you," Isabel said. "I guess I can understand why."

He stared at her, silent for a moment, then said, "This one will be really rough."

"You want to know something?" she said. "This one will be hard for me, too. I don't like the thought of leaving, and I'm mad at myself for ruining last night."

"You didn't ruin anything," he said, glancing at her mouth. "I knew asking you to move was a big request. And you had a right to be upset."

She frowned. Nodded.

"Maybe you should ask me to move to Kansas," he said, just barely lifting a corner of his mouth. "In the interest of sexual equality."

"Would you?"

"I don't know. I love my life here."

"I'll tell you one thing I do know," Isabel said. "We both love Sam and Darla, and we would regret doing anything that would tarnish their wedding day. Right?"

"Right."

"So, even though we're not exactly joyful, let's hold ourselves together," she said. "In fact, since we have only one more day together, let's make it special for us, too." She grinned. "Why, we could have fun with this. Maybe make wedding history!"

"You aren't suggesting that we skinny dip at the reception, are you?" he asked. "Because I can assure you it's been done."

"It has?" she asked, sidetracked.

He nodded.

"Well, no. That wasn't my idea. I think we should make tomorrow a first for *you.*"

The dimples lined up, and Isabel laughed. "I think we should make tomorrow the very first time that Trevor Kincaid actually enjoys a wedding."

"Think that's possible?"

"Why not? Sam and Darla planned a short ceremony, which will be followed by good food, drinks and great music. Sounds like a party to me."

He nodded. "And you will still be here."

"And I'll be here."

As they got up to leave, Trevor said he would be following her car to the ranch. He knew he'd be needed to help Sam in the morning. He'd brought an overnight bag and he was staying at the lodge, in his old room.

He paused near their vacated chairs, looking at her for a moment. She caught his unspoken communication.

He didn't *ask* her to visit him in his room; yet he did. With his tone and his expression and his soul.

She would make this last night work. No tears.

Chapter Fourteen

An hour later, Isabel met Trevor at his lodge bedroom door and kissed him before either of them had spoken. She didn't stop kissing or loving him until the wee hours, when they both fell asleep.

She woke in the morning, realizing they hadn't talked last night. And she didn't feel like talking to him now. She didn't know what to say and was becoming more and more miserable about leaving.

He woke up then and rolled over on top of her. Their lovemaking was slow and tender. Surely their final goodbye.

Then when the sunlight was strong across the windows, Isabel held her tears long enough to say goodbye to Trevor and sneak back to the house.

She allowed herself one good cry while she showered and dressed. Then she made her appearance in a kitchen full of happy chatter, and was immediately recruited to help set the reception tables and run folding chairs out to the gazebo.

At a little after three, Isabel, Darla and Darla's mother closed themselves into Isabel's bedroom to work on their hair and makeup. A knock sounded at the door a while later, and Isabel opened it to Trevor.

The ladies laughed at his reaction to their big curlers and green mud masks. "The caterers arrived and asked where to set up the buffet," he said. "Sam didn't know, so he sent me to ask."

He eyed Darla as if his friend would be horrified if he saw her in such a state, and the women all laughed harder.

He was adorable—playing it up, having fun and getting into the spirit of things, as he'd promised.

Isabel would miss him like anything.

Moving away from her family and her home to be with a man didn't sound right.

But leaving Trevor didn't feel right, either.

She wished her choice were easier.

At four-fifteen, the women heard another knock on the door. This time Sam walked into the room without an invitation, causing Darla to gasp, grab her wedding dress off the bed and run into the adjoining bathroom.

"I'm sorry, Darla. I know I'm not supposed to be in here," Sam hollered after her. Then he turned his worried face to Isabel. "But I thought you would need to know. Angie has arrived in her flower girl dress."

"She's here?" Isabel slid one last curler out of her hair. "Where?"

"She and her dad and her brother are talking to Trevor in his lodge office. You'd better get over there."

Darn right she should. Isabel glanced at Darla, who was peeking through the crack in the door. "Don't worry," Isabel said, soothing her. "I'll be back as soon as I can to finish dressing."

She rushed from the room, barefoot and still in her robe. When she strode into Trevor's office, she caught a glimpse of him in his tux before Angie jumped up from the long bench.

"Hi, Izza-bell! I gedda be the flower girl!"

The little girl was pretty in her delicate lilac dress, but the wrinkling near the hem indicated that she'd probably worn it all the way here. "I see that," Isabel said.

She said hello to R.J., dressed in his Sunday clothes and sitting next to Angie on the bench.

The she focused on Roger at the end. Handsome, pink-faced Roger, who'd worn his best blue suit.

"Hi, Isabel."

She shook her head. "Roger, what are you doing here?"

"I was invited." He pulled the photocopied invitation from his pocket, as if she'd asked for proof. "Angie wouldn't stop talking about the wedding, and we all missed you. So here we are!"

"I'll be heading home tomorrow, and you didn't tell Darla you were coming."

He shifted uncomfortably on the bench. "I know."

"We gave the caterer a head count a couple of weeks ago. Your showing up here isn't good, Roger."

"We don't need to eat."

That wasn't the point.

Trevor was standing behind his desk, watching her. She turned her gaze to him, taking in the rented black tux and those watchful eyes.

Isabel was amazed at the difference in her reaction to the men. When she was near Trevor, she bloomed.

Damn it. She'd wanted to prove to him that they

could do something different and end their relationship in a loving and creative way. She'd wanted to enjoy this day with him. She'd convinced him, and herself, that they could have a good time.

A bearable ending.

That was the point.

Isabel grabbed Roger's coat sleeve. "Follow me, please." She led him through the main office, then out onto the porch. Once there she turned to face him. "You should have warned me that you were coming."

"I called last night. There was no answer."

"We were at the rehearsal dinner."

"Oh. Well." Roger fumbled with something in his inner coat pocket, then slid down to one knee as he pulled it out. "I was a fool, Isabel," he said. "I need you to know that I still want to marry you."

He opened the box to reveal a diamond ring that he couldn't have afforded.

Isabel had her back to the lodge. She stood looking at a gorgeous ring and praying Trevor couldn't see or hear them. He'd be crushed.

She sighed and closed her eyes briefly. Finally she opened them and tugged at Roger's sleeve again. "Get up, Roger. This isn't the time or place."

He frowned toward the lodge windows. "Because of him?"

"Because this is Darla's special day. Not mine."

He closed the box with a snap and stood up. "But we will talk soon?"

"Not today."

"Do you mind if the kids and I stay?"

She sighed heavily. "I could hardly tell Angie to leave, could I? She arrived in her flower girl dress."

"That was her idea, not mine."

"And she's your kid. Ever think of saying no?"

He gave her a look of apology, then returned the box to his pocket. "R.J. and I will stand up to watch the wedding. Will you help Angie with what she needs?"

"Of course."

Isabel made it through the ceremony. She said and did all the right things, even chuckling when one of Angie's rose petals fell on Darla's aunt's lap and the little girl paused to pluck it off and toss it to the ground.

But she felt numb.

Darla and Sam spoke their vows beautifully, and they wore bright expressions when they were presented to their loved ones as Mr. and Mrs. Burch.

After Isabel had forced friendly chatter through the receiving line-greetings, she met Roger and the kids in the lodge and told them to go ahead and eat. She was certain that the caterers had brought enough food for three extras.

Besides, she wouldn't be eating. She suspected that Trevor wouldn't, either.

She found him talking to the minister out near the gazebo. He noticed her approaching and shook the man's hand, then met her on the path.

"Come with me," he said, and led her through the trees to the place near the riverbank where the raccoons had stolen their breakfast.

"I'm sorry about Roger," she said as soon as Trevor

had stopped and turned around. "I didn't know he was going to show up."

"I could tell."

Trevor shocked her then by kneeling down in front of her and pressing his face against her belly.

She held his head. "Trevor?"

He looked up, his eyes dark. "I know this is going to sound crazy and incredibly late, Isabel, but let's get married." He paused, then murmured, "I don't have a ring, but suddenly I have no doubts at all."

Isabel wondered if it would ever strike her funny, that two men had proposed to her in the space of an hour, and she'd felt miserable about it. "Trevor, you're asking me because you think you have to," she said.

"No, that's just it. I saw through the window, Isabel. I saw that guy get down on his knee and I knew I'd do anything to be in his shoes. It struck me that I could be."

But if he hadn't seen Roger on bended knee, Trevor wouldn't have thought of proposing. That didn't sound like abiding love. It sounded more like jealousy. "Trevor, stand up."

He frowned, and she bent down to kiss that gorgeous, thoughtful forehead. "I love you, Trevor. I think I always will, but I can't stay here." She whispered, "I need to go home."

He nodded. Then he hugged her for a moment without kissing her.

Taking her hand, he led her back to the lodge and then vanished through the small crowd.

Isabel stayed at that reception until it ended. She

helped Darla whenever necessary and stood with the single ladies for the bouquet toss only because Sam and Darla had pointed out that she was the only single lady present who was over six and under sixty.

When Sam's two elderly aunts missed the flowers, they landed smack in Isabel's arms. She handed them to Angie and went to help the caterers distribute cake.

The party dragged on, and she caught glimpses of Trevor but never spoke to him again. After a couple of hours, Isabel waved Sam and Darla off on their honeymoon, told Roger and the kids she'd see them at home and went looking for Trevor. Someone said he'd left to take a couple of Sam's relatives to the airport.

He'd never even said goodbye.

Four days later, Isabel was home and surrounded by the family she loved so much. Callie had driven in from Wichita with her son, Luke, and Josie had stopped by, too. Callie and Isabel were crouched down in the backyard garden, harvesting tomatoes, while Josie played with the little boy in a nearby dirt patch.

"You haven't talked much about your trip, Izzy," Callie said, setting a tomato in a bushel basket. "What's up?"

"She's in love," Josie said, just before she pushed air through her lips to make a motor sound for the toy dump truck she pushed toward their nephew.

Callie's eyes probed Isabel's. "In love? With the law professor?"

Josie paused her sputtering long enough to say, "That'd be the one."

Josie knew?

Since she'd been home, Isabel had told her only that she'd had a nice summer, and that Darla had been a happy, pretty bride. She hadn't answered questions about whether she had actually gone to bed with the man, and whether or not the *L* word was spoken, in bed or out.

Josie hadn't asked about those things, either.

Isabel felt her big sister's stare, but she kept picking plump red tomatoes and putting them in her basket.

"You are in love, aren't you?" Callie asked.

She shrugged. "So what if I am?"

"What happened, hon?"

"I'm wondering that myself," she said. "I meant to go help Darla and entice Roger to propose. I did all that, and Roger actually showed up at the wedding and asked me to marry him."

That had been just days ago.

The honeymooners were still in Alaska, for heaven's sake. But it seemed as if it had been ages.

Tired of squatting near the vines, Isabel plopped down on her bottom between the rows. "Actually, the law professor proposed, too. His name's Trevor Kincaid."

"He did? Isabel! Why didn't you tell us?"

This was Callie. But Josie had stopped playing with Luke and the trucks and was listening intently.

Isabel hadn't told them because she had always relied on her sisters to give her advice. But she felt as if she'd changed now. She was thinking differently, wishing she could call Trevor and talk to *him* about it.

She didn't think that was a good sign.

She missed him more and more, and she thought about him round the clock.

"I wanted to figure things out for myself," she finally answered.

Callie sat down near Isabel and picked up her left hand, checking for a ring. "You said no to both of them?" she asked.

"Yes." Isabel shrugged. "Actually, I didn't say no to Roger. He rescinded his proposal. He dropped by a few days ago to check on me, and he said it was obvious that I was pining away for the other guy. He claimed he couldn't marry me under those circumstances."

"Good for him," Callie said.

Apparently upset by his aunt's diverted attention, Luke kicked his heels on the ground and started making motor sounds.

Josie grabbed a truck and sputtered again, and Isabel watched her sister and nephew play.

They all loved Luke dearly. So far, he was the only child in the family. She'd thought that maybe Angie and R.J. would become a part of it, too.

"I feel awful about Roger's kids," she said.

"They aren't losing anything," Callie said. "Not with you living down the road from them. Just continue to be their friend."

Isabel nodded. "I will."

Callie studied her for a moment, then added, "Or even if you move to Colorado, you can telephone or write to them, exactly as you will with us. You can see Roger's kids when you're here to visit us."

"I can't move to Colorado," Isabel said, frowning.

"Why not?" This was Josie.

"I'm too much like Mom, I guess. I've always lived in this house. I like family. Quiet pursuits."

"Oh, puh-leeze," Josie said. "Mom convinced you that you were a homebody because she liked your company and wanted to keep you near."

"I can't count the number of times you've said someone was lucky because they got to travel or live out an adventure," Callie added.

"Those are only vague dreams." Isabel smiled.

"No, that's who you are, hon," Callie said. "Mom wouldn't have wanted you to pursue a life away from her. She did tell you, over and over, that you were quiet. Shy. Like her."

"All true."

"Uh-uh," Josie said, frowning. "You love us, I know. But you're no more a homebody than I am."

Isabel stared at the tomato plants.

"If you could do anything you wanted, with no thoughts of shoulds or only-ifs, what would you do?" Callie asked.

That was easy. She'd marry Trevor. She'd go rock climbing on weekends and help with the camp and spend every night in his bed.

In coming home she'd done exactly what her mother would have done. She'd chosen to keep her world small so she could control it and keep herself safe.

But on the day that she'd climbed with Trevor, she'd felt a real euphoria. If she'd never done it, she wouldn't have known what she'd missed.

But she had. She'd climbed the rock face.

And she'd learned to love a big-hearted man. A man she respected a great deal.

Now that she knew what it was like to reach for a

bigger dream, she didn't think she could be satisfied with a lesser one.

Isabel gazed at her sisters. "What if he doesn't welcome me back?" she asked. "I said no to him. I thought I needed to come home."

But she heard herself, and before either sister could say a word she said, "Shh. Don't answer. I've been silly, haven't I?"

She stood up and patted the dust off her pants, then sighed at the tomatoes and the garden and the house.

"Josie?"

"Yeah?"

"You want Mom's house?"

"What? You're giving it to me for good now?"

"Yes."

"All right! Party house."

Isabel joined Callie in laughter.

Eleven days later Isabel had done it all. She'd contacted her clients, paid her bills, packed and said her goodbyes. She flew to Colorado, rented a car at the airport and drove straight to Trevor's place.

It was a Sunday, so she knew he might be out. But since she'd arrived late in the afternoon, she hoped she'd catch him. She knocked, then stood away from the door when she heard footsteps inside.

He was home!

He opened the door, looking sleepy and sexy and wonderful. "Isabel?" he asked, opening his screen and stepping onto the porch in his bare feet. "Isabel?" he said again.

Her heart pounded as she watched his expression change from disbelief to curiosity.

"Why are you here?" he asked.

"I was in the neighborhood," she said, loving his half smile. "I'm moving here, actually."

He frowned. Gorgeously. How could she so adore a man's frown?

"I thought you could help me find an apartment," she said. "I've never moved before, but I've heard that it can be hard to go to a new town and find exactly what you want right away. Not before you know the place well."

The whole time she'd talked, he'd stared at her, nodding as if he was considering the problems of moving. Then he said, "Come on in."

She followed him in but stopped in the doorway. The butterflies had attacked. She squelched an urge to tackle Trevor and claim a few of the kisses she'd missed.

If things went well, she'd get to kiss the man all the time.

"I asked you to marry me," he said in a pleasant tone, as if he was informing her about the cost of an apartment in Boulder, "I meant it. Shouldn't you be moving in with me?"

"You asked me under duress."

"Maybe," he said. "But you taught me something, Isabel. Something that fifty percent of brides and grooms must learn."

She frowned. "Which fifty?"

"The ones who make it."

She grinned, then sighed. And kept listening.

"I figured they must find someone who becomes their best friend," he said, taking her hands. "Someone who is willing to listen fully or talk honestly, depending on what is needed at the moment." He gazed into her eyes. "They must have *this*. This bond." He squeezed her hands, giving them a little shake.

She nodded, "I think you're right," she said. They dropped their handclasp and she stepped farther into his house. "When did you figure this out?"

"Not long after you left," he said. "Actually, I've been planning a trip to Kansas. I thought I might check out job opportunities for law professors."

"Really?"

"Oh, yeah. You beat me to the punch."

"Well, I'm glad did, because I like the idea of living in Colorado. I never thought I'd say this, but I'll move in with you, Trevor."

"The small-town girl would become my live-in lover."

She shrugged. "Yes."

"What would your mother say?"

She grimaced. "You don't want to know. She wouldn't be happy."

"Neither would I," Trevor said. "I want to marry you, Isabel, as soon as we can arrange it. I want the right to have you next to me in bed every night. I want you to get really large with my babies, and then help me figure out what to do with them."

She stepped into his arms. "I was hoping you'd say that," she murmured against his neck, just before she turned her face for one of those hot, sexy, memorable kisses.

"Is that a yes?" he asked when he could.

She said it was, then kissed him again, then shrieked

when he picked her up and carried her down the hall to his bedroom.

While they were lounging between red silk sheets a while later, Trevor mentioned that he thought they should find a bigger place so she could set up Blume-crafts, if that was what she wanted to do.

"That sounds great," she said. "And you know, since I run a home-based business and you work a university schedule, we could take part of each summer to travel."

"And you'd help me with the summer camp? We could direct it as a team."

"Of course." She'd thought about doing a couple more sessions—set them up for teenage girls. "And we could visit my sisters often and invite them here?"

"You bet."

"You'll have to teach me a few things." Isabel sat up next to the headboard, excited by her thoughts. "Fishing. Horseback riding. And I'll want to go climbing all the time. I want to get good at it."

He scooted up next to her, matching shoulder to shoulder and knee to knee. "You'll learn fast."

"And, Trevor?" She leaned against him, felt his arm encircle her waist. His palm rested against her hips, and she pressed a hand over the top of it.

"Yes?"

"Let's save some time for *this*." She snuggled closer and gave his hand a squeeze. "For keeping the bond strong."

With his free hand, he touched her chin, then nudged her face toward his. "That sounds like the best idea of all."

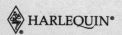

Signature Select™

A good start to a new day…or a new life!

National bestselling author

ROZ
Denny
FOX

Coffee in the Morning

A heartwarming volume of two classic stories
with the miniseries characters you love! A
wagon train journey along the Santa Fe Trail
is a catalyst for romance as Emily Benton and
Sherry Campbell each find love.

On sale March.

The story continues in April 2006 with
Roz Denny Fox's brand-new story,
Hot Chocolate on a Cold Day.

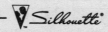

SPECIAL EDITION™

BRAVO FAMILY TIES
Stronger Than Ever

**THE IRRESISTIBLE BRAVO MEN ARE BACK
IN *USA TODAY* BESTSELLING AUTHOR**

CHRISTINE RIMMER's

THE BRAVO
FAMILY WAY

March 2006

The last thing Cleo Bliss needed was
a brash CEO in her life. So when casino
owner Fletcher Bravo made her a business
proposition, Cleo knew it spelled trouble—
until seeing Fletcher's soft spot for his
adorable daughter melted Cleo's heart.

THE F RTUNES OF TEXAS: *Reunion*

**Coming in March…
a brand-new Fortunes story
by *USA TODAY* bestselling author**

Marie Ferrarella…

MILITARY MAN

A dangerous predator escapes from prison
near Red Rock, Texas—and Collin Jamison,
CIA Special Operations, is the only person who
can get inside the murderer's mind. Med student
Lucy Gatling thinks she has a lead. The police
aren't biting, but Collin is—even if it is only
to get closer to Lucy!

**The Fortunes of Texas: Reunion
The price of privilege. The power of family.**

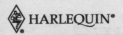

ternoon. She might even query his intentions regarding her friend.

When he'd sent the counselors away, he'd meant to follow them to town. He'd meant to check on things at home and rest up for the first week of camp. That was what he usually did on any off days.

But he'd seen Isabel sitting at the pool, and he'd been unable to resist. He'd changed into a spare set of trunks and plunged right in.

As he worked with Isabel on her float techniques, he decided he liked the idea of teaching her to swim, just so he could schedule more time with her.

In fact, right now, he had this strong hankering to kiss Isabel. A real kiss that had nothing to do with the camp kids or his crazy idea.

He moved his face nearer to hers, wondering how she'd react.

"Hey, Izza-bell!"

Isabel turned her head to look at the little girl. "What is it, Ange?"

"When you talked to my daddy, did he tell you the same thing he told me?"

Isabel offered Trevor a coy, "isn't she cute" smile before returning her attention to Angie. "What was that, hon?"

"He misses bofe of us, tons!" Angie's shout caused Isabel's smile to vanish. "We'll show my meanie brother. You're gonna be his ee-bil stepmother, too!"

Isabel bit her lip, giving Trevor a look he recognized. As if she'd been hiding something. As if she was doing something now that she shouldn't be doing.

Except, wouldn't that be presumptuous?

I know you're sort of interested, but don't fall for me because I'm sort of taken. Or I will be taken, if my make-Roger-miss-me plan works.

Sounded presumptuous to her.

Isabel wished she could talk to her sisters about all this before anything else happened. She knew what they'd say, though. Josie would tell her to have fun. Callie would warn her to be careful.

Maybe she could do both.

Maybe she should find out what it was like to spend time with an attractive member of the opposite sex whom she hadn't dated for three years, and whose routines and reactions weren't completely expected.

Trevor was scary. Serious. Exciting. He might be too much for a novice flirt to start with, but Isabel liked the idea of taking on a bigger challenge.

As he moved her slowly across the surface of the pool, she gazed up at him. "I like this."

"I do, too." His low, sexy voice sent tremors shooting down Isabel's body. But she wasn't cold.

Not at all.

Oh, yeah. She wanted to tackle this challenge.

So far she was having a blast.

TREVOR TUGGED his armful of wet woman into deeper water, thinking his idea to attach himself romantically to Isabel was working better than he had expected.

But he wanted to evade Darla, who might very well demand to know why he hadn't left for home when the counselors did, an aim he'd stated to her only this af-